Not Much Is As It Seems

Not Much Is As It Seems

Navniit Gandhi

Disclaimer

There are several stories, sayings, and sketches of people mentioned in this book, which I have simply read or heard somewhere and shared. I have quoted and re-produced them since they appealed to me. I am grateful to all the official sources from where the anecdotes and examples or wise words must have emanated.

I apologise that I am unable to mention/acknowledge the original writers/sources.

Published by
Ocean Books (P) Ltd.
4/19 Asaf Ali Road,
New Delhi-110 002 (INDIA)
e-mail: oceanbooksindia@gmail.com

ISBN 978-93-92963-09-4
NOT MUCH IS AS IT SEEMS
by Navniit Gandhi

Edition
First, 2023

Paperback Price
₹ 250.00 (Rupees Two Hundred Fifty only)

Cover Design: Helen D'souza

Printed at
R-Tech Offset Printers, Delhi

Dedicated to

all those friends and family-members who, and circumstances which, did not turn out as they seemed to be...

Preface

Hoooooof...phoooofff f!!!

It is huffing...and puffing; panting and gasping for air!

Yes, life is under heavy pressure... Or, do we, owing to *tuning* and habit, frantically search for reasons whereby a heavy load of pressure lands on our heads?

How does it all begin? When are attitudes and thought-processes formed? How and why do we look at ourselves and at others, the way we do?

At the first wail of a new-born, followed by the first-time holding and caressing by the loved ones—somewhere in that instant itself, a heavy load of expectations falls on every just-born baby!

Nobody says it, or perhaps no one is aware of the churning happening inside but an unseen, though humungous pressure of expectations descends and shades the aura of the new-born child. Our brain is wired such that all parents want their babies to always be happy, successful and healthy. Nobody wishes that may the child deal well with sorrow, disease, and failure! We just blissfully ignore the other side of the coin. And thus, life starts...

From the first day itself, we start fervently praying that: may *our child succeed; be happy; be beautiful; excel and be amiable, social, healthy and ambitious!* All of it generates a lot of pressure that is of course, not initially visible for some time. The hapless parents though, begin expecting fast and furiously. They all claim to love the baby irrespective of how the physical features or the colour or the mental faculties turn out to be, but deep down inside, they desperately desire all growth and development to be *perfect* and hopefully, exceed the *'standards'* prescribed in our societies.

Moving on from looks and health, the expectations grow bigger and heavier, as years roll by. The child must learn just the right things at the right time and then,—must not just learn but learn better and faster than all other kids around him or her. The child must excel in all that he or she takes up; be well-mannered and courteous; obedient and happy; ambitious and mature and of course, liked and appreciated by all.

With each passing year, the burden of expectations keeps getting heavier.

However, we never take a pause and ponder on: how were we trained and what was the outcome of that training, and how do we *tune* our children?

At every step, certain fixed ideas keep getting ingrained in every tender mind. A growing child learns to look at life thus: *difficulties are bad; tears are bad; failure is bad; not doing anything is bad; being alone is bad; being not liked by everyone is bad and so is being poor or ordinary*!

A child spends the first few years of life, in trying to

grasp what is what—followed by fulfilling expectations as laid out first by family and then by the rest of the world. Then, he or she handles his or her own pile of expectations from *self*; experiences a few bumps; gets knocked-out intermittently and then spends the rest of his or her life in wondering a lot!

- ✓ *What is this that has happened with me?*
- ✓ *Why do I have to face all these struggles?*
- ✓ *How could he or she behave thus?*
- ✓ *Is there anything such as justice in this world?*
- ✓ *Why me? Oh God, why me?*

Largely, we live non-plussed.

Some of us then grow weary and cynical by the time the wondering ceases. Some of us become fatalistic and attribute it all to *destiny*, while some of us choose to keep trying to amass the *best*.

Well then, how does one shrug off the expectations and live reasonably well?

While one eternal truth is that there is no one who has led or will lead a ***perfect*** life! Hence, to begin with, let us agree that a reasonably well-lived life is what we are looking at!

Proceed with caution if you aim for the stars! Yes, there are stars and geniuses who have defied gravity and have dazzled at peaks, but this book isn't for them. This book is for you and me; for us who are bestowed with moderate, almost frugal amounts of skills, sanity, desires, and dreams.

Are you game for living with minimum fuss, cynicism, and vanity?

This book is also not for anyone who expects other

people or others' experiences or books and lectures by others to solve all their problems in life. It is also not for someone who expects that one day, there will be no problems to tackle.

If you are an average person who started off with a little grasping and gradual understanding of people and situations, and then a little bit of dreaming, followed by facing challenges; tasting moderate failures and even smaller successes, and then wondering a bit about what is life and how the journey can be well-lived—then just keep reading...

Contents

Chapter 1

Are YOU At Ease?

You shall need a pen and a sheet of paper...

To note: *Do you experience, at least once every day, a total sense of ease within yourself? For how many minutes and/or hours in a day do you, on an average, feel at ease? Do those carefree and at-ease minutes, arrive at approximately the same time daily?*

For instance, I feel most relaxed and carefree, when I sit with myself for breakfast and hold my first steaming cup of tea, with all the chores having been completed by then. It is that first slot of moments when I am at ease; when there is sunlight streaming in from the window; there is silence; space; tea; food and often,—an engaging episode of a series to watch on television!

Well, how many such moments do you manage to experience, in the course of one day? If there are plentiful such moments when you feel light and warm; relaxed and pleasant (for no specific reason) and the mind resembles a tranquil lake rather than a stormy sea—then, you have done your bit and are living well.

If there are sparse or no such moments, then let us endeavor to do something about it.

To begin with, it happens to be quite an established truth that nobody can feel at ease all the time. It is just not possible.

A self-professed and widely-famous Guru, who is a good orator and holds his audience captivated with his witty jokes and one-liners in English says in one of his videos: 'Life is all about making choices'.

He adds: 'while anger comes naturally, to be calm is a choice; negativity is natural, but positivity is a choice; and disliking is spontaneous but liking is a choice.'

I mulled over his lines. I do understand what he is trying to say and appreciate the message.

But I wonder whether we ought to make these constant choices all the time? To be happy; to love; to like; to agree; to be positive—and all of such choices? Why shun half the emotions and embrace the other half? Surely, this is no way to usher 'completeness' or 'balance' in life! Such imbalance can also be potentially toxic. Have you come across someone in your life, who always smiles; always laughs; and is all the time chirpy, positive, excited and happy? Don't think we would like such a person. It would be impossible to always be with such a person. He or she would seem unnatural...

Let us ourselves try for a week. Let us try to make all the correct choices: to be positive; to be compassionate; to be forgiving; to be generous; to be loving; to keep smiling; and to like everyone and every situation.

I have tried. Am not much evolved yet perhaps, but didn't feel great. Felt tired and worn out. Felt as if I was carrying an artificial load.

I feel it is best to flow with the tide. It is alright to sway with the breeze. I feel it is alright to feel a little envy at times; a little anger at certain people and state of affairs; and that a little whining and a little selfishness is all fine. When I say 'a little', it is here that a 'choice' surfaces. You must make yours and I must make mine. For you, based on your life and its circumstances, how much selfishness or anger will be healthy, you must decide. I may choose to whine for three days, while you may choose to do it for 3 hours! If I choose to grumble for half a lifetime, I would upset the cart and miss the point. Which emotion and for what duration and in what intensity is healthy for me—that is the one 'choice' which we must make for our respective selves.

It is crucial to be 'alert' so that we are able to recognize that one moment when the balance could be disturbed and the good might turn ugly.

Let us not choose to embrace just one half and discard the other half of emotions.

Let us make just one crucial choice: which emotion shall occupy how much space in our being and for how long!

A tranquil lake too has to have a few ripples now and then. Or, it would be a dead one. Feelings of anguish, worry, frustration and restlessness will visit every mind at routine intervals. Whether you allow them to visit or not, they shall do visit. If you are prepared, and have chalked out a way to observe, understand and embrace them—well and good! If you live in a denial mode or are boastful that you remain calm and positive all the time—you shall experience a steeper fall and find yourself stuck in a quagmire for a longer time.

To live well, it is important that the visitors not be allowed to become permanent residents. It is then, that a range of physical, emotional and mental challenges spring up and forever threaten our inner peace.

How does one feel at ease?

It starts with the body. If the bodily functions are regular and smooth, half the battle is won! For a person who is unable to pass urine or stool normally, the millions in cash or stock; the luxuries; the jewelry and all the other gleaming possessions shall bring no joy. Physiologically, and in fact, ultimately in life—this is what really and crucially matters: *whether a person can eat, digest, sleep, and excrete normally or not*! These constitute the essential foundations on which then, we can breathe easy.

Of course, it also matters whether one can walk, get up and lie down, see, hear, speak and do what and when one decides or wants to. It is not that those who cannot, are unable to feel at ease, but what I mean is that the pertinent reasons to worry, then cease. Strange, isn't it, that millions of us whose bodies are able to do all of the above-mentioned physical tasks and the brain is able to do the mental tasks normally—still find little gratitude inside ourselves and fail to heave a sigh of relief.

A man who had lost both his legs in an explosion, was invited to give a motivating speech to a group of university students. At the end of the speech, a student walked up to him and said with a cynical expression: 'How do you manage to stay positive, when you have no legs?' The speaker replied with a slow smile: 'Well, strange that you manage to stay negative, when you have both yours!'

A person who is not able to eat or pass urine or sleep fitfully, will find no joy in any number of luxuries. First and foremost, is good health. We can never be happy without that. All ailments will keep deducting from the joys that we may otherwise try to amass. At the same time, however, sound physiological functioning is no guarantee that you or I shall have the sensibility to appreciate its worth and shall feel light inside. If we are not aware of how big a deal it is to be able to stand, sit, walk, talk, eat and breathe at will—we can never be at ease.

During the corona pandemic, the importance of being able to breathe naturally, without external oxygen supply, dawned on us. The pandemic gave us some very important lesson for us to value life and our loved ones. Our hearts should have been filled with gratitude, while also with guilt at many hitherto insensible ways of ours. A giant sense of realization was expected to blow over us and sweep us off from where we stood on pillars of vanity, but alas! We didn't realize much and didn't change our ways much either.

These are the two basic ingredients, thus, for feeling at ease:

✓ **Physiological well-being**

✓ **A sense of contentment deep inside**

If you lack the former, there are ways to cope and recover from ailments. Much also will depend on how soon we realize what wrongs we are committing and how soon do we take the reins in our hands for taking good care of our bodies.

But if you lack the latter, there is no way you can buy or borrow and then plant that contentment inside you, unless and until life itself teaches a few lessons and in the process, the seeds of contentment are planted inside. We may read books and listen to motivating sermons by life-coaches but if the very seed of contentment is not there inside, it won't be easy to cultivate the feeling further. A bit of it, at least, has to be there in our persona; lurking there somewhere in our hearts. If a *desire for more* is always tugging at your sleeve and your core being stays forever discontented, then feeling *at ease* and living life in one's natural stride will be hard to come to you.

TO SUMMARISE: to be at ease is the most essential condition to live well. This state of being is needed to be able to look at life—a little *beyond the obvious*. And, in order to be at ease, there are two requirements: one, that our *body functions normally* and we are largely in good health, and secondly, we remain *grateful and contented* with what we have.

Without these two pre-conditions, the mind will always be restless, irrespective of what you are able to gather and amass for yourself and your loved ones. And if your mind is restless, you shall not be able to look at the real picture or look *beyond what seems to be* there...

Let us assume that you had a little trace of contentment; that it was a part of who you were when your journey had begun, and that as you began to aspire for *more*—you completely lost all strands of contentment. It will still be possible then to re-discover yourself and pick up the pieces. Do know that feelings of discontentment are not just with reference to materialistic things but even with respect to people, or systems or thoughts or just the state of being. Even if you are a very contented person as far as worldly possessions are concerned, you may still be discontented at the political system or the prevalent practices in the society.

Worse still is if we are discontented with our own selves. It is much worse than being discontented with what we possess. For, if it is all about materialistic possessions, the chances of we realizing our follies one day, are bright and many. However, if there is a nagging unhappiness with our being; if there is a self-eroding *self-doubt*, the efforts needed to reach the stage of being *at-ease*, shall be humongous.

Dealing with self-doubts

Well, do you doubt yourself?

I occasionally do, and I am not ashamed to admit it...

There are several folks I have come across, who never doubt themselves; not even for a moment. While I admire some for their self-confidence, there are others who come across as too self-assured and arrogant. I, then, heave a sigh of relief, glad that at least I am not pushing people away from me due to this over-bearing *self-assuredness*.

What about you?

- *Do you doubt yourself, in the sense that you are not too sure of whether what you think, speak and act is or isn't good enough?*
- *Do you keep quiet when you know that you must not, just because you are not too sure of yourself?*
- *Do you wonder a lot about why and how are others so very talented and confident?*

If it is a 'yes' to all three of the above, then while we need to sit up and do something, we can also pat and comfort ourselves because we aren't alone in this battle with doubt. Self-doubt has plagued the minds and persona of many a top-achievers too. A lot of successful and famous personalities have spent sleepless nights afraid that they did not deserve all of what they have achieved and that it shall all be taken away.

Maya Angelou once admitted: *"I have written eleven books, but each time I think, "Uh-oh, they're going to find out now. I've run a game on everybody, and they're going to find me out."*

The thought that they are not competent, despite the success and fame, gives a lot of anxiety to many of those whom we actually admire in our lives. When taken too far, a mild and harmless feeling of self-doubt makes the hosts feel that all of their name and fame is a fraud. Known as ***Imposter Syndrome***, these disturbing thoughts can rob us of all joys and contentment in life.

Why not ask our best teacher: ***our own inner self***, as to why and how did these self-doubts began to occupy precious space in our hearts? The causes behind these nagging feelings that *I am no good,* are largely owing to the atmosphere at home. We are certainly not born with these fears and it seems that much depends on how the initial raising of a child has been. Well, since that is not now in anybody's control, let us look at what can be understood and dealt with:

- **Looking outside rather than inside**:
  If there is a streak of **comparison-with-others**, *inside us, we are likely to keep looking outside at what others have got, much more than we look inside at what we've got! This certainly aggravates self-doubt because there are a lot of good and capable people out there. This constant comparison must stop! If our parents have done it, it is bad as it is but, if we too do not quell this habit soon—it may overwhelm all our thoughts and make us afraid-to-act all the time.*
- **Unpleasant Experiences:**
  Some of us start confidently on a blank slate, but then one **unpleasant experience** *blows that confidence to pieces and we begin doubting ourselves. For instance, if any of us were mocked at for giving a wrong answer in the class or were laughed at, for our looks or were ridiculed for thinking in a certain off-beat way—we may shut-up forever and withdraw. Deep inside, we start questioning all that we are and only a good friend or confidante can then apply the brakes and restore the confidence...*
- **A fiercely Competitive Environment**
  An unsuccessful episode wherein we fail at an exam or in an interview or fail to get a much-deserved scholarship, pushes our confidence to rock-bottom

levels and we begin wondering if we are good at anything at all or whether we deserve anything good at all! The competition all around us for positions, jobs, seats, scholarships and opportunities is so very intense that it is not possible for us all to win. Some will lose.

- **Fear of Losing**

  Why do successful people suffer from doubts and complexes? Well, after having had a brush with success and fame, their fears and insecurities grow even bigger, for they are now afraid of losing it all one day. They hold on like a baby—to what thin and thick strands of success they have. Sometimes, they know that there were and there are more meritorious folks who didn't get it all, and deep inside they feel guilty about what they could amass for themselves.

Well, am no expert but I do feel that it is important to remember that: ***it is alright to be afraid; to be unsure and to wonder if one is saying and doing the right things...***In fact, a little doubt might propel growth and learning and inspire a drive towards excellence in us.

Yes, it is normal to be afraid.

The goal ought to be to not let these doubts grow beyond proportions so much so that they threaten to derail everything.

WE CAN:

- ✓ **At first, let us take good care of our body. Even if you doubt that you are not good enough, it is ok. Do not take part in competitions or do not voice your opinions if you do not wish to.**

Exercise well. Eat healthy. Let your mind and body be at ease.

- ✓ **Take good care of our mind. Even if we are busy in doubting ourselves, we can spare a little time and read good books; meditate a bit; watch good stuff on TV and even laugh a bit with friends or with oneself. Do not battle with your doubts till you feel you are not ready. But till then, just work bit-by-bit on your body and mind.**
- ✓ **Decide to spend time only with folks who make us feel good. Those friends or family members who constantly cry, complain or crib can be kept a little at bay for some time. We can do this for some time, till we have first handled our own affairs.**
- ✓ **When self-doubts start nagging, it is important to break that chain of thoughts immediately. Get up and go for a walk or switch on the TV and watch your favorite sitcom or grab a healthy snack and pick up a hilarious book. Call a friend who talks frivolous gossip all the time. It is important to break the chain.**
- ✓ **Accept that a little bit of self-doubt is healthy and hence we are normal! It's just that we have to keep such thoughts from getting too severe.**

Do these feelings ever go away?

Yes, they do!!!

To have one good confidante who listens, understands and loves unconditionally can make the whole difference.

Being absorbed in an activity that defines you, such as gardening or cooking or writing or painting—helps too. This is an issue which cannot be tackled directly and at one go. These feelings of self-doubt slowly recede. When we spend time with people who sincerely and silently urge us to go on, we surge forward step-by-step and leave these feelings behind.

That crucial sense of ease will keep eluding us as long as these feelings of discontentment, self-doubt, and frustration keep scrambling for a permanent place in the being.

Let us keep walking...We surely shall meet good friends on the way. And one day, when we look back—we shall find that we have been shedding traces of self-doubts while enjoying the walk!

Well, it surely is the right time to:

Grab the tools and get going...

- ✓ **Breathe Easy. Focus on your inhalation and exhalation and remember that it is just a *breath* that decides whether one is alive or a corpse. Sit down to breathe deeply and gently as often as you can. It changes attitudes gradually...**
- ✓ **Accept that you won't have everything that you desire. No one has! Live with a few empty/blank squares. Do not scramble or go overboard trying to keep your bundle full and that too, with only the desirable goodies.**
- ✓ **You yourself are a mixed bag. Perfection is an illusion; a mirage. Stop hankering after perfection in yourself and in others.**

- ✓ **Most important: THERE IS NO PERSON ON THIS PLANET FOR WHOM LIFE HAS TURNED OUT TO BE EXACTLY AS HE/SHE HAD PLANNED IT OR DESIRED IT TO BE!**

When the 34-year-old World's no.1 tennis player (as in January 2022) Novak Djokovic set out to travel to Australia for adding a 10th Australian Open title in his kitty and thereby breaking a 20-Grand Slam singles record, he never must have thought in his wildest imagination that he would be deported from the country he is travelling to!!! At the worst, he would have anticipated a setback on the court but not the unleashing of a saga mired in controversy. His iron-willed resolve to break the record of 20 Grand Slam singles record was as strong and unbeatable as his 'form' was. Everything was at its place: the plan; the dream; the capability; and an amazing and impeccable track-record. And yet, life had its own plans. The world's no.1 found himself embroiled in controversial lapses, omissions and errors and twice sent to a detention center and eventually deported.

- ✓ **Just look all around you very carefully. Do it as often as you can. And try to look deeper; beyond what is very apparent and obvious. A lot depends on whether we are willing to be patient and if we are good observers. It is usually from nowhere, that life suddenly springs the most joyous and meaningful experiences for us.**

It is precisely then—when we grab the above tools and set forth that we find life rushing towards us with open arms, with all the thrills and frills it can muster along with.

I have often felt bubbles of pent-up angst, pain and questions about how Nature and this society is blatantly unfair towards women. Just to live fairly and squarely without even once being inappropriately touched by someone or once being reminded by someone that she needs 'permission' at some point of time or the other in her life—is itself a struggle and often, one with unsuccessful outcomes. On one such day when the rising bubbles were causing turmoil inside, I decided to pen down my feelings in my blog-post.

However, even after pouring it all out, the heaviness persisted.

And then, the very next day, as I sat sipping tea, I got a nudge.

A friend forwarded a link to a write-up by Maria Popova on brainpickings.org which quoted Bruce Lee's famous metaphor for Resilience: "Be Like Water."

The article left me in a deep trance. It kind of melted a huge boulder of cynicism somewhere inside me.

The writer quotes from the Book: Bruce Lee: Artist of Life 'which is a compendium of his-never-before published private letters, notes, and poems and which offer insights into his thoughts'.

After a period of frustration with his inability to master "the art of detachment" which his only formal martial arts teacher Yip Man was trying to teach him, Bruce Lee writes:

"My instructor would approach me and say,"... preserve yourself by following the natural bend of things and don't interfere. Remember never to assert yourself against nature; never be in frontal opposition to any problems but control it by swinging with it..."

The writer describes that how Lee spent many hours thinking and meditating and one day while sailing alone in the sea, he got mad at himself and punched the water! It is at that moment that the turning point came for him. He realized that while he struck the water, it did not get hurt; it wasn't wounded and though water seemed so weak but when he tried to grasp a handful of it, it was impossible. Water may have no color or shape or its own distinct identity for whether one places it in a tea-pot or in a huge vessel, it takes that form—and yet as the writer points in the article: 'when heated to the state of steam, it is invisible but has enough power to split the earth itself. When frozen, it crystallizes into a mighty rock...'

Yes, isn't it true that whether water is turbulent or calm or whether it gurgles playfully when it is a brook—the point is that it flows... It accepts and it flows.

The writer further quotes Lee: "This was exactly what Professor Yip meant by being detached—not being without emotion or feeling, but being one in whom feeling was not sticky or blocked."

Just as the moment must would have been a nudge for Lee, the experience of reading about it, was the nudge for me. "Be Like Water"—the words struck right through and I felt as if I shrugged the Atlas. The words kept ringing and I realized the utter foolishness of me trying to question Nature or pass judgment on Creation and of blaming the Creator as unfair... I felt foolish dwelling on truths beyond my comprehension; felt foolish at me trying to label, conclude, criticize, get angry at—while not having probably seen a grain of the vast universe.

To accept it all with ease and live in a state of natural flow... to adapt...to accept...to feel detached—all of it, I know, will not come in a day. But the nudge has broken the reverie soaked in self.

Sometimes, it is all that one needs to wake up; to *shrug the Atlas*; and to drop the unnecessary, heavy and stale load that we carry and trod along painfully. Yes, a *nudge* is all it takes to shrug it off and to feel light; to feel at ease with oneself.

And then, we move on...

□

Chapter 2

There Are Always Several Stories

Lurking just round the corner, there are always too many stories; just too many stories.

Not much in life can be taken at its face-value. When a husband complains about his wife or a wife does the same; when a tragedy strikes a family; when a friend says he was betrayed by his bestest one; when a tale of courage or valor is told and re-told—there is always a web of tales lurking behind each narration. Even when no one is narrating but there is just an event that occurs—the need for a pause is imminent as *what seems to be, is often not so!*

The story of an old Chinese farmer who lived many years ago, has been told and re-told for generations now:

Once upon a time, there lived an old farmer in a small province of China. He had one old horse that he used, to plough his fields. One day, the horse ran away into the hills. Everyone said: "We are so sorry for your bad luck." The old man was wise. He calmly replied:

"Bad luck, good luck, who knows?" A week later, the horse returned with a herd of wild horses, which now belonged to the old man. Everyone said: "We are so happy for your good luck!" The old man replied: "Good luck, bad luck, who knows?" While his only son was riding one of the wild horses, he fell off and broke his leg. Everyone said: "What bad luck!" The old man once again refused to label the occurrence as good or bad luck. He calmly replied: "Bad luck, good luck, who knows?" One day, the army came to the village, and took all the strong young men to be soldiers for the emperor. Only the old farmer's son was spared, because he could not fight with a broken leg. Everyone said: "What good luck!" The old man was quiet for a moment or so. But then he quietly replied: "Good luck, bad luck, who knows?"

Behind every situation that stares at us; behind every person we happen to meet; behind every scene that unfolds; behind every trait that we apparently like or dislike—there are just too many stories.

Haven't you felt this truth at some time or the other?

Remember those times when you met someone whom you thoroughly disliked the first time, but the very next instant or in the next few days or months—a story, hitherto lurking in the shadows, came to the fore, and your perceptions and experiences changed instantaneously?

Let me share a personally experienced anecdote:

Was rummaging through the drawers the other day, and lo, behold...a memory fell into my hands; a memory carefully preserved of someone's identity.

Guess, memories are the best reminders; the best teachers and in case we forget our lessons—they bustle in with a force and command you to sit down and take note of the forgotten lessons.

It was 15 years ago.

Newly married, I came to Kuwait. My better half already had a modest social circle of friends and acquaintances—all of whom had to be given a wedding treat.

Arrangements were made. A nice, warm party was thrown for about 100 guests (30-35 families). I was introduced to many folks whom I had not hitherto met. It all went very well...

The next day, we excitedly began opening the gifts. Although in a lighter vein, but a spate of reactions we gave, one after the other. There were exclamations; there were sighs; there were Ooooooo0s and Ahaaaaas and Ohhhhhs...Ours was going to be a fresh start in a new household and many gifts were directed at that fact.

Towards the end of the thrilling session, we found that there were three gifts with no names mentioned on them. We made the calculations quickly and found that there were three families which had come and given us gifts but they were not accounted for, in our list of who had given what. So, there were 3 mysterious gifts and there were three families—each one of whom must have given one of the gifts.

The gifts were thus:

1. *A beautiful idol of Lord Ganesha*
2. *A glass flower vase*
3. *An exquisite ladies' watch and a handsome shirt*

The three families were:

1. *An extremely rich and highly-regarded family, wherein the husband was the GM of a very reputed company*
2. *A modest middle-class couple, both of whom were professionals*
3. *A Bangladeshi family with whom a kind of affinity had built when the gentleman was given the job of painting our new house, before I arrived in Kuwait.*

The guessing game began. It didn't take us long to figure that the middle-class couple, who were also very devout worshippers of Lord Ganesha must have gifted us the idol. And obviously, we thought that the General Manager and his family must have given us the watch and the shirt.

We called up everyone in the evening, and thanked them all for their presence, wishes and the gifts. Don't know why and how, but I recall that we were more lavish while thanking the GM's family. After all, the watch looked simply stunning and the shirt was of no less expensive a brand.

The discussions on gifts kept going amongst both of us for a few more days, and gradually other important things took over.

About eight months later, we got a call from the Bangladeshi gentleman, saying that his eldest son had scored 90 per cent in Class 10 exams. We congratulated them profusely and gave our best wishes for his future. In the next two days, we decided that we must go and give a small little gift to the child for this achievement.

On the way to their house, I felt pity for what must surely be harsh living conditions for them. The father did house-painting and they had three kids. Their building was not in good surroundings either. I recall feeling a bit patronizing in that moment when we entered their house, thinking that the poor family will be elated at our visit and at the chocolates we were carrying for the kids.

Everyone was undoubtedly very happy at our surprise visit. Shakila (the lady) insisted that we have tea. The husband rushed out and returned with arms full of vegetarian snacks for us.

While sipping tea, Shakila looked at me, and then at my wrist, smiled and shyly said: "I knew the watch would look beautiful on you."

Many more profound incidents must have happened with you.

It is our inherent tendency to take people, incidents, situations and life itself, as they appear to be. This very tendency is to be blamed for we not experiencing the *real* picture. Coupled with this tendency are our two traits of being excessively *self-assured* and *arrogant*—which cloud the vision further and we miss it all.

Rahul was the seventh child born to his parents. Unlike his elder siblings, neither was he good-looking (as the world defines) *and nor smart. Not much attention was therefore showered on him, during his childhood. He was largely dismissed by everyone in his family and though he did grow up—nobody knew how or when. His ordinary features and lack of any visible talents strengthened his belief that 'he just didn't matter'. One day, as he stood outside a store that sold old books, he instantaneously knew who his 'best friends' were going to be...*

All during the growing-up years,—from teens to adulthood, he had several friends (girls as well as boys). Because he had plentiful empathy, his was the shoulder all his friends used liberally. He knew the importance of giving and receiving love. His thoughtful demeanor attracted many girls towards him and he too used to like everybody in an affectionate and friendly sort of way.

To the world, it appeared that he was not steadfast in the matters of heart or of friendship because there were too many girls all around him, but he was beyond the mundane definition of what constituted 'allegiance', for he liked everybody he met. He was also quite modest a person. He didn't think too much of himself. However, a deep-rooted sense of gratitude for what he had, had made him humble. With not much love and appreciation from his family, he knew he had to carefully hold on to the meagre reserves of love he had amassed for himself in his life.

Anybody who happened to meet Rahul had his or her own perception of him; had a distinct version to narrate. Some labelled him *fickle-minded* in matters of heart, whereas some others saw him as that *empathetic* one who could never break hearts!

However, the reality is that there are always too many layers: not just to people but also to the happenings in life. Even for an occurrence as simple and straightforward as *death,* and the mourning that accompanies it—there are simply too many stories. Each one who is connected with the departed soul in one way or the other, not only has a different story weaved with his or her grief, but the intensity of the mourning felt and displayed, also varies and holds many an untold tales.

BEHIND...

...every mother who appears selfish or uncaring to her child

...every father who appears disinterested to the children

...every seller who appears sweet and reliable

...every friend who seems aloof and unfriendly

...every child who appears bashful and angry

...every delinquent who appears remorseless

...every lover who betrays

...every actor who is a comic and makes everyone laugh

...every player who breaks down in front of the spectators

...**there are countless stories.**

"Remember, there are always two sides to every story. Understanding is a three-edged sword. Your side, their side and the truth in the middle. Get all the facts before you jump to conclusions."

—J. Michael

Even when we enjoy joy-rides in an amusement park, and the gushing adrenalin makes us forget all the cares in the world, not many of us pause and think of the several stories that must have graced or disgraced the making of the park. As for example, the mangroves that would have been destroyed or local communities displaced or trees cut to build that park for our amusement. Whether we make the effort of unearthing stories or not, the fact remains that the stories are there. You may wonder: *of what use is this attempt at trying to know the hidden stories*? Well, a big advantage which accrues for us is that it slows down our presumptuous tendencies and makes us less judgmental. Weaker the judgmental streak in us, stronger shall be our vision and sensitivity. We could become more empathetic and the world could thereby become a little bearable!

Just as every old man or woman who is sitting on the road or on a bench in a park, in a disheveled state, with tears in his or her eyes, is not necessarily a beggar seeking a few coins, so also every successful person soaked in luxuries isn't a *'whole being'* inside. Once we understand this, not only shall we gain much personally, but also become sensible and caring folks.

Once it so happened, that on a fine sunny day, there was a private bus packed with worshippers, going on a pilgrimage. The temple was atop a steep hill and the passengers were keen to reach the destination before the sun set. They stopped briefly at the base of the mountain, and then resumed the journey hurriedly before it turned dark. The bus had barely gone a few meters ahead when all of a sudden, dark clouds appeared from nowhere, and roared thunderously. It began to rain heavily. The sky turned black and the visibility dropped. The bus continued to inch forward, though the passengers were horrified at the sudden fury unleashed by mother nature. They did not want the bus to stop despite the rumbling and lightning. Every few meters, the bus would shake and lose balance, even as it precariously trotted ahead on the rocky path. The pilgrims started praying and furiously moved the beads back and forth, even as their fingers shook with fear.

"One of us is certainly a sinner, and he or she has aroused the wrath of God. Clearly, *God* is upset with us", a voice shot out in the bus. Everybody turned to look at each other, stunned. The authoritative male voice rose again: "Let us stop the bus every few meters and one at a time, one amongst us get down for a few seconds. Clearly, when the sinner gets down, the bus will move smoothly ahead and we shall all be safe." It seemed worthwhile and everyone murmured their assent to the proposal. Meanwhile the storm was raging madly and raindrops were hitting the window panes with a deafening roar. The bus was wobbling so badly that it could plunge in the gorge below, any moment.

The man with the authoritative voice got up and staggeringly reached the driver and instructed him to stop the bus every few meters. One passenger at a time got down from the bus, and the bus inched forward. If there was no change in the conditions, the person would run along and board the bus again. Then, the next person would get down...and that is how it went on till everybody had alighted for a few seconds and then boarded back. Finally, the one who had suggested the idea got down the bus and jogged along with it and was about to get inside again when he spotted a movement on the roof of the bus.

He shouted that the bus be stopped and climbed up the roof—to find a beggar woman crouching at one corner of the roof. She was in rags and drenched. On being found out, she began to tremble like a leaf. Apparently, she was cold and panic too had seized her. The man began to shout mercilessly at the woman and dragged her down. Everyone came out of the bus and stood in the downpour, looking disgustingly at the culprit who had put all their lives in danger.

There was no dissenting opinion. 'Of course, she is the reason why *God* is upset with us. She seems to be a thief and God knows what other sins she may have committed in life. Let her perish here in the rain and we shall ask for forgiveness from God for having unknowingly brought a sinner at His door-step. Let us continue with the journey,' *was the unanimous verdict. The woman pleaded and wailed, but it was all in vain. She said she wanted to go to the holy place to pray for her ailing son but since she had no money to buy the ticket, she was sitting ticketless on the roof. Nobody wanted to hear her cries. They cast a look of disdain at her and boarded the bus.*

The bus had barely gone 50 meters ahead when it hit a boulder, shook violently and fell in the gorge below, killing everyone instantaneously.

Moral: The bad deeds of someone had not placed everyone's life in danger, but the good deeds of one had kept them going and alive…

We cannot just form a final opinion of a person or a place—based on a single story we have heard or read.

There is a tendency though, on our part, to label people of specific religions or regions or nations with certain good or bad adjectives. There are always *'several' stories*. Ironically though, it is because our minds are fickle and operate irrationally most of the time, certain vested interests have used this weakness of ours to form opinions and prejudices based on hearsay or on a few apparent episodes and have thus spread ugliness in the world. They have succeeded because they know that we won't go deeper; we won't look beyond what is apparent or stated and we won't look at the other *several stories*. Many a cunning folks play on this widely prevalent weakness and make us all an easy prey to their ugly agenda.

A message drafted/created by someone out somewhere, reiterates that: *'yes, there are always several stories and not much is as it seems'.*

- ✓ *If a person laughs too much, and even at stupid things, he is lonely deep inside.*
- ✓ *If a person sleeps a lot, he is sad.*
- ✓ *If a person speaks less but speaks fast, he has secrets he is keeping well.*
- ✓ *The person who brings out the best in you and makes you strong, is actually your weakness.*
- ✓ *The one who cries on little things, is innocent and has a tender heart.*
- ✓ *If a person becomes very easily angry over small or even petty things, it means he or she needs love.*
- ✓ *Those who cannot cry, are very weak inside.*
- ✓ *If someone eats in an abnormal manner, he or she is tense.*

To live life to the fullest, we very often need to unravel the layers and know the stories. Doing so shall enhance our capabilities; our understanding and our perceptions of people, incidents and circumstances that engulf us.

Even with national and international issues, there are always several stories. For example, if five sensible scholars sit around a table to discuss: *what and which is the real India*, a debate shall inevitably commence. Such a debate can possibly go on for days, with tempers flying high but towards no clear a picture. It is just not possible to emphatically say that *this* is the true and the final narrative of India. While some may rant on the greatness of our civilization, others could angrily point out the lack of a national ethos and dispute the claim to greatness.

Even in the case of a war between two nations—the winner will have a different story to tell, and the loser, a different one. In fact, more often than not, there are not even clear losers and winners and therefore, one forms opinions by looking at or listening to heaps of complicated stories on which the broken societies and nations rest!

Forget the past, but even with respect to something that is going on right now; right in front of our eyes—it is impossible to state that *this is the final story*. And this is true, despite the impeccable and incredible strides made with respect to technology.

Sometimes, there are too many stories and knowing this fact, we want to take a peek *beyond the obvious* but, the layers are so very beyond our comprehension that we give up the unravelling part.

Even if you or I cannot see the stories or read the

hidden message or unfold the mysteries of life, we can at least wait and watch the stories unfold with time. The highly-strung or the temperamental keep making pronouncements at will, with a loud bang: *that, yes, life is superb or life is hell or that the present times are miserable for all or that this is ill-luck and that is good-luck...*

Of what use is all this rhetoric? Why this unbridled tendency to presume hastily?

Such attitudes simply push us towards diseases, or despair or both, even as we harbor dim and dark views about people and life.

I recall an experience when I had inferred hastily, only to regret later:

One of our professors in senior college was not very regular when it came to engaging classes. She remained absent most of the time, and even when she used to come to the classroom, she sounded dull and disinterested. We were an enthusiastic bunch ofyoung learners, but also impatient. We found her to be very mediocre, and developed a severe dislike for her. We made fun of her in the classroom (in her presence), and even played pranks many a times. I even wrote a small column in a newspaper somewhere that why and how anybody was allowed to become a teacher, just on the basis of some paper qualifications, though such teachers ruined the interest of thousands of students in a particular subject.

After completing my post-graduation, I got a job in the very college where I had been a student. I found myself seated in the staff-room amongst my own teachers. While it felt good to be amongst familiar faces, it was also awkward to sit face-to-face with that one teacher, whom we had troubled much and propagated against. She apparently had no clue that I was one of the pranksters or that I had even written against her in a newspaper (without naming her). She was so happy to see that one of her students had joined the college as a lecturer, that she went out of her way to make me feel comfortable. She was still irregular in coming to college, but whenever she was there—she would smile at me lovingly and ask me if I was doing well. Some four or five of us, including her—used to have breakfast together in the staff room. When she came to know that I loved the sweets and savories she made, she began getting extra helpings for me. Within a few months, I found myself liking her immensely and warming in her company.

One day, I overheard a few teachers talking about that teacher in her absence. I was stunned to hear that she had cancer and that how it had spread to all parts of her body and how she was struggling to survive in the last stage. I asked a few other teachers about what I had heard, only to know that she was battling cancer for seven years. I came to know that she had a daughter as small as 12 years old and that she was very much worried about her. I felt dizzy with shame, as I recalled those days when we had smirked at her discomfiture in the classroom. She was probably undergoing chemo/radiation sessions during those times and her mouth would have been all bitter and body reeling under the harsh treatment. And, we had made fun of her, imitated her and even instigated students against tolerating incompetent teachers.

I came to know from batches senior to ours that she had once been a very bright and enthusiastic teacher who deeply cared for her subject and her students.

I did what I could to make up for what I had shamelessly done. In whichever way I could, I tried to ease her load; wrote cheerful cards/notes for her when she stopped coming to college altogether, and visited her at her residence as and when I could. She succumbed to the illness soon thereafter...

I learnt from that experience that the conduct of a person tells us only a bit of the whole story. What a person thinks; does in other situations with other people; what his or her past is, and what bruises are hurting inside are other sub-plots and when they reveal themselves, even the most adept story-tellers can find their heads spinning in disbelief!

Whether a person is gregarious or is incompetent or plain stupid—that one dimension of the person is not the one and the final story.

Yes, wait we must and observe carefully what life offers to us as it unfolds bit by bit...

But, shall we modify the *watching* part a little? Let us not watch through a keyhole this time; let us not see just a part of the big picture! Let us not see just how much we make or how much can we gain or acquire and possess; and let us not, through a keyhole, look intently only at our worries. Our planet may be a tiny blue dot, but we are smaller and even more insignificant and hence, this world is relatively too big for us. There is a lot to see and admire. One lifetime will not be enough and certainly not so if we keep watching through a keyhole.

What say?

Shall we open the door this time and take a full

overview? Let us not crouch and fearfully peep to know what lies outside. If the world is too big for us, the joys and tears too are too big for us to fully fathom. For many of us, we just do not get the time to see beyond us; to see beyond the keyhole...We remain bogged down with our own affairs and mostly, with our trivial affairs.

This time, not through the keyhole then! There are too many interesting stories out there, waiting to fall in our ears and nestle in our eyes.

Open the door wide. Look all around. Perhaps, we shall see and listen to some fascinating stuff; understand what is *beyond the very obvious*. Perhaps, when we open the door wide and peer closely, we shall be able to see beyond the dark clouds and happily spot the silver linings in the sky. Perhaps, as we open our door and step outside, and we see the dark clouds hovering over strangers or our loved ones—we shall be able to open our umbrellas just in time...

□

Chapter 3

Dilemmas and Decisions

Did I do the right thing?

Was my choice correct? Ought I to have made that decision?

Did I err in opting for what I did?

Should I call him? After the way he has cheated on me?

Is it worth going on in such an unpleasant environ?

Dilemmas! Dilemmas!

Dilemmas—big and small; relatively easy to resolve or impossible to solve; occasional or every now and then! A lot of lives are grappling with dilemmas all the time. Wrapped in dilemmas thus, it becomes difficult for us to choose and make decisions when perplex situations confront us.

A helpful lesson (if only one can learn early) in life is: that **there is nothing whatsoever as the *ideal* or the *correct* decision**. Yes, it is all a matter of timing and our conduct after a decision is made. Either before making a decision or even after making one, it would help tremendously if we are conscious of this truth that *not much in life is what it seems to be*!

One of the most oft-experienced dilemmas which

I have found myself and others wearily staring at, is *whether to give a second or a third chance to a relationship after the other has cheated or betrayed or let us down.* When a blow strikes us in a dearly-held bond, it hurts quite a lot; quite a lot indeed—as if the heart is slowly pierced into and torn apart. When we are so very fond of someone or emotionally dependent on a loved one or have placed unflinching faith in a friend, the dilemma which confronts us is whether to break-off or to ignore the stabs and keep going on? Either way, being in pain seems to be a certainty.

But, hey, just take a pause for a moment...!!! Often, *it is not what it seems!* The pain which one feels could very well be the gateway to better and brighter times. The loss could be the prelude to a lot of gains in the offing. Perhaps, we haven't understood the cause well or the context maturely. Perhaps, the other person is a victim of circumstances himself or herself; perhaps, destiny brought him or her as a facilitator of good times in your life.

An old story that I had read somewhere some time went thus:

Once upon a time there lived a warrior king who loved hunting and was quite adept and ferocious at that. He always was accompanied by his pet falcon who was equally brave and fearless. The falcon could see far and beyond and often proved to be useful to the King in his hunting expeditions.

One day the king and his companions went on a hunting trip deep inside the jungles and spent the whole day searching for preys. However, the whole day they couldn't lay their hands on a good prize. Everyone was exhausted after spending an entire day in scorching heat and humidity. They decided to call it a day and returned to their camping site. The king, however, was frustrated and spent a restless night. Next day, early in the morning—the king took off on his horse, along with the falcon. He went galloping far and soon got lost in the jungle. The morning turned to noon and the king realized that he had not any food or water with him. He was tired and thirsty. There seemed to be no source of water which hadn't got dried in the severe summer. Just as he thought he would collapse, the king happened to hear the gentle sound of trickling water falling from amidst the rocks. The king was mighty relieved. Just as he bent down to scoop some water in his palms, his favorite falcon flew with lightning speed and overturned his palms and the water fell down. The king looked up at his pet and wearily thought that perhaps the bird too was thirsty and hence had behaved weirdly. The king again managed to collect water in his cupped palms and was about to bring it to his lips when the falcon again rushed in and overturned the water. This time, the king became a little angry and looked at the bird pleadingly.

The third time, the king tried again to drink a few drops, the falcon attacked again and the water was spilled. Enraged, the king took out his bow and arrow and aimed at the falcon. The arrow pierced the bird's body and it collapsed on the ground with a loud cry.

The king was in tears but desperate for water too. As he turned towards the water, he found that the drops had dried down and no water was coming down the rocks. The king decided to climb up a bit and see if there was a pond or stream from where the water had been trickling down. As soon as he climbed up the rocks, he was stunned to see a poisonous snake lying dead in a small pool of water near the rocks.

The king was dismayed. Had the falcon not thrown the water every time and allowed him to drink, the king knew he would be lying dead too.

In the desperate moments of thirst and exhaustion, the king had failed to see *what was beyond* the bird's apparent attempt at spilling the water.

Haven't we too, on several occasions, accused people or yelled at our own folks for doing something or saying something what we then felt was totally unacceptable? We have said harsh words to or been mean with many because we felt that they were coming in the way of what we wanted; what we were pursuing. Just as the king pierced the falcon's heart, we have done so with many a loving folk.

If we really wish to avoid such traps, we can:

- ✓ either be just a little patient before we conclude and at least make one attempt to look ***beyond what is so apparent.***
- ✓ or accept and flow with the consequences of what others have done and wait for life to unfold the mysteries.

Women who are victims of domestic abuse, are usually tormented with a difficult dilemma: *to keep going on in a toxic relationship or to call it quits?* When we come across such a victim, we are angered looking at their plight and wonder as to *why is she being such a weakling? Can't she just separate from such a spouse?* However, there is much *beyond the obvious.* It is never too easy. It is often not a matter of will. Every woman in India or even worldwide, is not so blessed even today so as to have any assured rights to inheritance. Not everyone has her own home to go to or to claim as an inherited right. Even if one decides to just remove oneself from such situation of violence, the question remains as to *where to go to*?

One might argue that *why not earn and manage somehow?* However, not all dilemmas are so easy to resolve.

Smriti was a very beautiful 17-year-old when she fell in love with a boy from a different religious denomination. The parents had raised her very protectively. When they came to know of this affair, they stopped sending her to college. She was made to enroll in a distance-learning course and somehow graduate. There was no exposure to the real world and nor any skill-acquisition. When she was barely 20 years old, her parents took her to their relatives in the USA and got her married to the first guy they thought suitable.

Her husband turned out to be a compulsive alcoholic and a gambler. They did not have children. Six years later, the husband died. Smriti was at a loss, regarding what lay ahead. Parents did not want her to return to India. They searched frantically and got her married once again to a prosperous Indian-American business-man from the community.

She soon found that this time, she was going to have to suffer from a different kind of domestic abuse because the husband was practically a semi-literate chauvinist who expected an obedient but pretty slave who would cater to all of his needs. Smriti soon gave birth to a boy and thought that a child could perhaps change everything for good. Her life changed, but not the way she had hoped for it to. Alas! The little kid was born with severe autism.

Today, the kid is 13 years old but unable to walk or express himself and is therefore completely dependent on care. Smriti has been living a nightmarish life all these years, knowing that continuing the marriage—would mean that all of her kid's needs for therapy, medicines, food, and the like would be well taken care of. She thinks that if she walks out of marriage, she would collapse under the weight of taking care of a kid with special needs. She is not equipped with any skill-set, needed to survive and sustain herself and her differently-abled child. Yes, we may perceive the situation differently but it is her take on her situation!

In her own words:

'I'm good. I'm as good as *good* can be. Physically I have mostly everything (food, clothes, home, car, etc.).

Emotionally there is a lingering worry. But I've learnt to tune that out too. I distract myself & consciously choose not to think about it.

What I cannot change why worry about it.

I'm still thankful to God.

I've never really had money problems ever.

We take vacations, buy cars, bills are paid. My son also gets everything money can buy from his father and what money can't buy—from his mother.

Life is not perfect.

Thankful for what I have.

Hopeful for what I wish to have.'

Whether between two people or between two courses of action—dilemmas always keep us unnerved. We struggle to weigh the pros and cons and thus, choose. We always hope that we end up making a good decision; a logical one. However, one can never say!

Is there a formula whereby dilemmas can be successfully resolved?

No, there is no formula or prescribed method of resolving dilemmas (though I, very often, resort to tossing a coin, when I can think no further). And the priority ought not to be to make the *best* or *correct* choices and decisions. No one can claim to do that all the time or even most of the times. No, that isn't and ought not to be the concern. What ought to matter is attuning ourselves sensibly, when and while looking at the consequences of the decision made.

Sometimes it happens that we sit tight and not do anything and the matter passes. Usually, we have to choose. And every choice shall entail consequences. It is how we look at the consequences and respond to them—that ought to be our concern. If the response is *guilt* or *anger* or *frustration* or *regret*, we spoil our precious years most stupidly. It is so because sometimes, an entire life-time goes in resolving these feelings of guilt and regret. And all of it is to no avail. Yes, none...

No one can foretell what dilemmas shall present themselves in our life-time. Though some of us are proud of our prowess at planning in life, life has its own ways of asserting itself to the contrary. And then, we find ourselves face-to-face with dilemmas. They always bounce right at us from corners, least expected. After tormenting ourselves for days and nights, we make a decision. And then, if at all, our calculations go wrong—we wring our hands in despair. It is here, at this point, that sensibilities are called for.

Does it all really happen for 'good'?

An important truth to remember here is that contained in a very cliché statement: ***it all happens for good!*** Yes, it does. If at all there is no good coming out of it, then—well, that is how it was supposed to be! However, more often than not, after a little digging here and there—one discovers that *good* which is not too visible all the time. If any scene, at any point of time in life, looks all bleak or even all rosy—that can never be the truth because *nothing usually is what is seems!* What usually is—is a mixed shade of colours. Yes, every time!

In the years I have spent in Kuwait, I have seen all around me very well-qualified women expats who arrive here in order to be with their husbands who were already working here or who got a job in this part of the world after marriage. There is almost no instance of a man coming here to join his wife and then searching a job for himself. The qualified ladies who immigrate here do search for a suitable professional placement in the initial few years. Some of them succeed too. The majority compromises while accepting a generic/administrative or a teaching position.

For a small minority though, their inability to get a regular job, proves to be a boon in disguise. They gather the time, their space and solitude and pen down their thoughts or turn to music or to dance or to creative business ideas. Have seen the creative juices flow mightily here in the desert nation. They are able to pursue a passion or effectively put their creativity to solid use, because they are not into any 9-to-5 jobs.

Of course, there are also those few who relax, and happily take a back-seat—enjoying life; and lavishly spending the dinars their husbands are making. And then there is a small segment of those too who ceaselessly crib and complain; fret and whine as to why life brought them to such a place!

A package-deal it always is!!!

The thing to remember is that nothing ever emerges out of feeling regretful or guilty. **Dilemmas will come and decisions will have to be made. But no matter what one chooses, life is inevitably a package deal!** This truth, if thoroughly understood, can usher much simplicity in life. No matter what decision we make or which course of action we choose, there shall be the black, white and grey shades. *The focus, needs to be correct, therefore.* Instead of *'over-thinking'* and being headstrong and trying to prove that we are in *'control,'* it would augur well if we gracefully *'accept'* what we cannot alter; if we put in our best and improve/alter what we can and if we never lose sense so as to know the difference.

Sometimes, it is about choosing what to ignore and what not to; or it is about which relationship to give more attention to; or even about whom to trust and whom to be wary of. All the time, we are making decisions—big or small. When one reaches the 30s, and one is no mood to take un-called for strain and stress, there are people and things that one gets weary of dragging along with oneself. There are people and things—which no longer give joy and seem to be just dead corpses. The mind definitely wonders: *what exactly to do? Ought we to bury such relationships or just keep pulling along?*

Till a few years ago, even I wondered a lot about those relationships which seemed to have just drooped on the way; wilted...and withered away. You too must be having your fair share of such folks. I found that my list of such ties that had drooped, fortunately or unfortunately, had expanded notoriously over the years. Several relationships seemed to be meaningless. I decided to just shrug. It feels lighter to just shed; to shrug the Atlas! Over the past year or so, I have increasingly been shrugging off the drooping lifeless bonds! I feel I wasted precious time in resolving this dilemma; in holding on to the stems, trying to keep them straight and it had been all in vain.

Parenting Dilemmas...

Parents, in particular, heavily reel under dilemmas: *what to allow and how much to allow what; what is good and what isn't; how tight to rein in and how much to let go and in what area...*You too must have seen innumerable instances of parents struggling to juggle between ensuring discipline, holding on to traditions, and fulfilling the incessant demands of their kids. They are an exasperated lot:

- *if gadgets and junk foods are bad, shall we force our denial on our kids and always see them sitting cross with us;*

- *should we buy comforts for them or not and how much is exactly too much then;*
- *should we forcibly make them learn prayers/ lessons prescribed by religious texts;*
- *shall we allow their peers to influence them or not let our kids develop bonds with their peers?????*

The list of questions never ceases to grow. I believe that the key lies in:

- ***the foundation that is laid in the initial years***
- ***the example that parents have set with their own conduct***

If kids find their parents healthy, happy and contented, the kids will surely emulate them at some stage or the other. If the parents get the kids interested in reading, music, listening to stories, adventure and outdoor activities, and in exploring the vastness that life is—I don't think kids are going to be cross at parents for not giving them play-stations, fries and burgers! It may seem that the teens in general lack focus, purpose and sense. However, everything is not exactly what it looks like. Kids are drawn towards the meaningless pursuits only in the absence of meaningful ones. It is a bored kid who is more likely to pick up gadgets or throw tantrums for having been denied junk foods.

When kids grow up—they encounter their own share of situations wherein they must decide and choose. But before those days arrive, wouldn't it be nice if we equip them with the basic sense that no matter what we decide, we must at first, ready ourselves to live with and accept what follows...? Our choices and decisions do tell us a lot about ourselves to others, but to us and to the quality of our own life—what matters is *our conduct* after the decisions were made and the dilemmas resolved. *How did we then behave, on looking at the outcome? How did we react when we saw what followed our choices...?*

Sadly, we are so caught up in our own mesh that we have no time to equip our kids with the skills that matter. We do not teach them the above and the scene is that young girls and boys are 'calculating' the pros and cons of choosing a career or of falling in love with A or B or C instead of relying on the musings of their hearts or on their *gut* feelings. Not many have been taught the art of bracing themselves for what may follow once the decisions are made. Hence, at the very first sign of aberrations in their expected outcomes—they break in pieces and sink in despair and depression!

I heard a mother once say this to her on-screen daughter in one of my favorite TV series:

'*There are lessons to be learnt all throughout from the moment we are born till we depart. Some of those lessons we learn on our own, and there are some which 'time' teaches us. However, it would be good if the most crucial lessons are learnt by us well ahead of time. For, if we wait for time to teach us all the lessons, the lessons may be too hard for us to swallow and even painful for us to bear because time always extracts a heavy price for teaching us those difficult lessons. And then, we have no choice but to pay that heavy price!*'

The pressure *to follow suit*, in whatever the world around us is up to, is simply humongous. The pressure to conform; to not be left behind; to surge ahead at the pace of the rest of the world and much more is clouding our vision. The result is that it is becoming all the more difficult to make decisions for 'ourselves'.

A dear friend, apparently concerned at my more than a year-long status of being jobless, kept keenly trying to hammer inside my thick brain-walls—the importance of being on a networking site. I listened to him patiently, nodded, hhmmnned, and then dithered, wavered, and opted to remain undecided. Unperturbed, I floated in the dilemma, for a couple of months.

At last, I decided to take a chance. I took the first step and created an account. I sifted through for a few minutes, but immediately panicked. Everybody was trying to sound important; everybody seemed to know everything and everyone and everybody's claims were bursting through the skies. I felt I was drowning in a sea of people who were all moving in giant waves—each trying to be heard, liked, appreciated, read, and known. I asked myself: In this plethora of cross-wires and connections, wherein everyone is trying to know or be connected with someone useful or well-positioned, where shall I stand? And, to what purpose?

I decided to take a pause, and withdraw.

This is my reality today; my decision today. Perhaps, I may realize that it was a huge folly, in the times ahead. Perhaps, tomorrow's reality could be different for me. I know not, what tomorrow holds...However, today, my mind holds peace inside.

I know several people who are neither very successful, and nor are scaling heights in whatever little they do for survival. But their hearts hold peace. They are not frantically expanding their network online. They cannot be seen in 'happening' parties, where important people are to be met, impressions bolstered and one's profile marketed.

Have you too experienced moments when one must choose between being practical or heeding to the silly cries of the heart? Well, what do you choose then? Rather, how do you make the choice? Think for a moment and take a glance at what has all of it brought for you...

Is it important to always decide; to plan and to choose?

The years when the corona pandemic altered the course of our lives, were a good learning experience for us all. In a way, every year and every day teaches much for those who are open to observation, contemplation and learning. During the covid years, the episode was one, and the experiences were largely of similar shades, but the lessons which we chose to learn, varied.

The futility of *making plans* dawned on us quite strongly, amongst the other truths. Only a few, though, realized that going berserk in calculating all our courses of action; making resolutions; and uttering solemn promises for a life-time, isn't a sensible choice. And sillier still is our supposition that methodical planning and calculations can solve all issues. Alas! Millions of us; in fact, billions of us had so, so much lined up and chalked out for the years that have just slipped by. Marriages were planned and travel itineraries were set and massive business-expansions plans were drawn—but all went awry. Nearly everyone had something or the other chalked out and yet, life caught us by surprise. Despite all the advancement in medicine and other sciences, a virus kept us contained, isolated, locked, and panicked and that too, not for a while but for almost two years. All those who had nefarious plans or any harmful agenda succumbed to the virus just as those who were going to make this world a better place with their benevolence, did. Many dilemmas were automatically resolved and an equal number of fresh ones born, just as decisions were made or overturned or crushed.

Irritants, issues, dilemmas, hurtful moments, plans going awry—and many more such episodes will always be sprinkled on the path where we tread. The key lies in how well do we ***Accept and Flow.*** There is just no need to decide most of times; and we needlessly break our heads and lose our calm. A much saner option is to calmly receive, observe what we have received, accept it and flow with the tide. I know this sounds cliché but this is it! Till that moment hits us individually, we may brush it aside as cliché, but when it hits, it seeps inside...

There are and will be a few moments when we must dream though, for the twinkles in the eye must not die altogether! And then, there ought to be a modest wish-list too. But the larger part of one day and one life, better be spent in training the mind to simply ***flow*** with the tides...

This attitude also may not be the ultimate truth at all times. Accept this calmly too. Nothing can ever be said with certainty and nothing can ever be labeled with confidence as ***the right*** or ***the wrong***. It is best to remain in a state of flow and flux.

□

Chapter 4
Seeking Is Dangerous

The speck of dust
The dust once thought that if she could ever fly
she would never come back to earth.
So, she prayed and meditated and chanted
and did all that was in her power
to make the Gods fulfill her desire.

And the Gods did listen.
The wind blew with such power
that it took the dust over the trees,
over the mountains, into the sky.
She travelled everywhere.

She felt she fulfilled her destiny.
The magic played on for some time.

But now...she wanted to return back n rest.
Enough of this travel, enough of this
sense of reaching somewhere.
Being this enlightened, self-awakened
dust particle, higher than the rest !

She wanted to be dust again.
She wanted to be...just be.
And she cried from the deepest core of her heart.
She cried till the Gods sent her back.

There back on earth, she rested like never before.
She realized she was always this.
Always perfectly herself but all that journey
to the sky and beyond, was perhaps
only to make her see so.
And how she smiled then.. looking at the sky.
It was amazing.

All her knowledge had dropped.
All desires had dropped.
She was once again, a nothing.
But within that nothingness
there was this amazing Grace,
The Grace of Being.

And she settled. She finally settled as she was.
No seeking, no searching...Just being, AS IS.

And then the winds smiled, the seeds dropped,
the sun shone, the rains showered
and flowers sprouted.
The dust had dissolved.
She was no more.
She had become All.

—**Author** (Unknown)

And, so it is with life. *Don't you think so?*

Is there really someone who truly understands what *Life* is? DO you?

Life and this Universe are such incomprehensible phenomena that we will not ever know what to make of them.

And yet, we jump to conclusions before we blink; we assert as if we know it all; and we embark on a crazy *wanting* and *amassing* spree, believing that all of what we seek is for our good!!! Nothing could say more about our foolishness than the latter!

All of it—this Universe/Nature or Existence if we may call it—all of it is so vast that we are not likely to catch a glimpse of even a speck of it. And here, we are...trying to not just alter its ways but also confident that we know it all and can run it better and must control it for the *good* of all!!! No other species of living beings display such an utter lack of sense, as we humans do most of the time, or rather, all the time. Deeply dissatisfied as we are, and full of ourselves, we have been on an endless rampage since thousands of years—trying to control land, oceans, other planets, women, animals, birds, children, glorious positions, wealth, the weak 'n vulnerable, socio-political and economic systems, jewels and all possible other lives and objects!!! We want to have it all; we want to own it all; and worse still, we want to alter it all because we think we know what is *the best course of action.*

We are all practically alike here. At some level or the other, we display the same tendencies and desires. A conqueror sets on a violent spree of annexation and plunder while you and I seek to control the lives of our kids and/or spouses and siblings. This streak of *controlling* is inherent. Whatever is possible within our limited sphere, we try and gain control of that.

What we seek may vary, but we do essentially and inevitably seek! Most of the other living beings, seek food and shelter for survival and then stay put. We, on the extreme end, go much beyond food and shelter and keep hankering after or chanting for or obsessively pursuing more and more wads of notes or jewels or houses or land or positions or an infinite spate of luxuries and brands! There is so much that we want all the time. In the present times, there are so many objects and things being manufactured, advertised and sold that this infinite bombardment of countless products is making our greed infinitely expansive too. There is just no end to how foolish and how dangerous we are turning out to be!

Can you imagine the other living beings, whether penguins or camels; whales or lizards; bees or elephants—shedding blood in order to loot Hermes handbags or racing to make a deadly nuclear bomb??? For none of the other living beings, life is one bit about 'possessing' things and going to the cruelest extremes for them. Also, no other living being punishes others so fiercely or even kills and loots in order to gather and be laden with luxuries. For survival, yes! They do kill. However, they do not kill more and eat more because there are days on which they feel like celebrating more or pompously displaying their might more or because *just like that* they want to hoard for their grand-kids!

Have you ever seen birds or animals praying for 'more'? Have you seen them making more nests than they need; gather more food than they need; or keep their loved ones sheltered for more time than is needed? They are all, since thousands of years, just one with themselves and with Mother Nature. We are making life difficult for them by threatening their sources of food, water and habitats. They, however, have not forgotten their essential and suitable diets; they haven't forgotten their migratory routes even as they recognize weathers correctly; they have not forgotten how much shielding their little ones need and they know whom to attack and when and how much food to seek.

We get more years to be on this planet than dogs and donkeys do, but we spend an entire life-time seeking things we are not going to carry or use, once breathing stops! Ironically, it is only at the very beginning and at the very fag end, that the original essence of life—'*survival*' prevails in our psyche. For a child, just as for a person beyond 80 years—only hunger, sleep and digestion matters. During these two phases, if you present property papers or locker keys on a platter of gold to someone, he or she may throw them back with a cry! However, the period that we live in between the beginning and end of life, is potentially destructive for self and others! It is in this interim period that we acquire notions such as: **'I know. I shall control. I want and I must have...'**

Our ego balloons unbearably during this period.

How much to seek? Rather, should we seek at all?

And then there is this crazy scrambling and wailing over what we seek, even as billions of us—at all moments that there are, fold our hands or spread them out towards the sky, clamoring and ranting before God to fulfill our wish-list. At every given minute, there are uncountable candles being lit and *diyas* being held before holy books or idols, and infinite demands being put forth. Often, we begin humbly, but as days and months pass to no avail, anger and frustration creeps in us as we angrily bash and brand everything as mighty '*unfair*.' There is no dearth of folks who agitatedly then become skeptics or atheists or even convert to another faith because they have *lost faith* in their own. Very few amongst us turn *inwards* when their wish-list lies unattended, and become even more staunch *believers* or try to modify the list instead.

There are not many memories of my childhood that are still vivid and fresh. Most are getting blurred and eventually blanked out. There is one memory, however, which is very vivid. I must have been about ten years old. The *Doordarshan* channel used to air a series wherein short stories written by eminent writers from all over the world were telecast. One day, there was this short story going on, and it left a deep impact on my psyche.

(The gist of the story I remember, but not the details—which I am therefore just making up myself)

Once upon a time, there lived an old widow who had one son. The son worked on an oil rig in the deep sea. He could neither visit his mother often and nor send her money at regular intervals. The widow loved her son very much. The sad grey eyes on her wrinkled face, carried anticipation, sadness and prayers at all times.

Once it so happened that several months passed and there was no letter or money that she received from him. The rent was due for several months and the landlord was no kindred spirit. He had threatened the old lady with eviction if he was not paid the rent in two weeks. The old lady was frightened. One day, a man selling junk stopped in front of the old lady's house and asked her if she wanted anything. The lady said 'no' but the seller persisted. Finally, he brought out an old monkey made out of wood, and told the lady that it was a 'wish-fulfilling' monkey. Anything that one asked of it, was granted. The old lady's eyes lit up for a moment and she told the vendor that since she didn't have any money with her, would he accept an old lamp instead? She brought out a lamp for him to see. It was a unique antique piece and the junk-seller was immediately glad with the bargain. He handed the wooden monkey to the woman and plodded along.

The old woman took the monkey inside, placed it on a pedestal, closed her eyes and began fervently wishing for $300 so that she could pay the rent amount. She wished hard and ceaselessly over the next one week or so.

One day, there was a knock at the door. The old lady opened the door to find a stranger standing outside with an envelope in his hands. He said: 'I work for the same company, in which your son worked. Four days ago, there was an accident on the rig and unfortunately, your son died in the fire. The company is very sorry for your tragic loss. I have been sent by the company to give you the dues payable to your son. The total is $300. Kindly accept the payment.'

Whenever I recollect the story, it always manages to send a chill down my spine.

It is not that one should not pray or not believe in God or not ask for what one wants. If it is in moderation, it is fine. The story made me wary of *obsessing* for what I want or *wishing too hard and too much.*

On several other occasions too, just as I have had experiences of miracles occurring and one being endowed with what one prayed for, so also there have been instances *when that which came true, came true at a price!* And the price was too tough!!!

Should we not Pray, then?

'Praying' to a higher power (if one believes there is and in whichever form one believes is in) is *submitting*. If we have faith in a higher power, then after presenting a wish or a desire, there has to be faith in whatever the outcome may be. Sadly though, here we have thousands queuing up on all days and at all times during days and nights—to 'seek' what they want. They feel let-down and angry; frustrated and agitated too if what they desire does not happen soon enough. With some, it barely takes 20-25 days for them to feel crestfallen and betrayed if God doesn't listen to and gives them what they seek! Aahaa! Vanity, thy presence is just enormous!

There is no harm in wishing or wanting a thing but then it is obsessing that is dangerous! Also, I believe that one ought to be wary of even 'asking,' for who knows what would it be like if it really happens that way. We could either miss out on something higher and bigger or simply end up paying a heavy price for what has come true.

An old acquaintance happened to hear a lecture by a motivational speaker and got convinced that there lay tremendous power in ***affirmations****. Lo, behold! In her own room, as well as in their kids' room—posters sprang up everywhere, depicting all that they sought from life. There were pics of a luxurious cruise ship she wanted to go on and* *pics of the houses/offices and other things that she and her family wanted. She even encouraged her kids to write down in notebooks, whatever they desired, over hundred times each. She herself began to write in a notebook:* ***'I have a good and reliable domestic-help,'*** *hundreds of times! Even percentages of marks that the kids wanted began to be jotted down in notebooks for 100+ times each. At the same time, their claim that they are devout worshippers of a particular faith, haven't waned.*

I once asked her: 'what if fate wanted you to go to Paris, Rome and Switzerland but you have been asking for just Egypt?' She kept arguing that 'one gets what one seeks, and that is a fact!'

Incidentally, the couple continues to fight over issues which have been the bone of contention for several years now. They argue over who shall do which household chore; who shall bear how much expense at home and whose parents shall have primacy over their domestic affairs. Their health issues have also multiplied, but their notebooks are getting heavier...

Every day, from the moment each one of us wakes up—there are dozens of desires and wishes that either keep cropping up in our minds or we verbally keep putting forth before the One we believe in. If each one's dozens of desires daily begin to come true, what would the fate of the world be! And the kind of stuff we seek is crazy and often, potentially very harmful! All of us want to live in joy all the time; we all want victories and good performances and successes in all that we do; we want our kids to be the brightest, best and the most successful and obedient ever and we want only happy and good times with and the best package deals from our life partners...and on and on!

Just imagine the chaos that would ensue if all desires of all of us are heard and they come true!!!

Then there is this other side...

Have you ever intensely sought a particular position in your career or ran after a much-coveted job? Or, gone nuts trying to woo the love of your life? Or, went crazy yearning for a house? Or, for a scholarship? Or, desperately prayed for your kid to get something he or she wanted?

Did you, then, get that job or the love of your life or that position or fame or success which you obsessively pursued? Did you? And then, what happened?

My experience says that anything which is difficult to get, becomes then even more difficult to keep! If several years of life and painstaking efforts have gone in trying to get a particular status or job or reputation or someone special's love—even greater number of years and more energy goes into not losing the same coveted *goal* that we acquired.

There are a few lives which, when I look at—I feel that they could have been *chilled-out* and pretty lives! But, alas! They are devoid of any joy or fulfillment because the first half was spent in intensely seeking something and now, the other in desperately holding on to that! And, whoooosh! At any moment, it could all be over!

All of us have indeed heard of celebrities, who got lucky in their initiatives early-on. Whether they won laurels with their first on-screen appearance or won medals and prizes in their maiden forays in sports or writers who got it all with their first book, the stress of maintaining that love, fame, success, wealth or whatever, remained till the very last moment they breathed!

What to do, then? Not to seek? Ever?

Even if we do not desperately pursue something we desire and just get it with sheer luck, it is not easy to cling on to the rewards. Sometimes, when I look at those who get it young: fame or star-status or wealth, I feel sad for what they may have to endure to make that fame last long. The entire lives of some of our celebrities seem to be a long struggle to cling to that star-status they acquired by chance or with diligent efforts.

Strange, isn't it, that we always seem to be rushing to go somewhere we are not, and seek what we do not have? Even after we get something we had sought, we continue seeking the other things we don't have and strive to go where we have not yet reached. Whether all of these quests lead us anywhere or not, is a matter very relative! We must thoughtfully choose what we wish to spend this life-time seeking and whether it is worth it! And also, be as much prepared for *fulfillment* as for *emptiness* at the end of the quest or worse still, for *dejection*.

Nevertheless, do take a long pause and think before you step out to seek. Being obsessed or obstinate for a job or a loved one or for a position or for an amount of money or luxuries will certainly entail a cost! Are you prepared to pay the price?

Am wary of the outcome of all that which happens even on dating sites. Young boys and girls are obsessing over finding 'someone' to hang out with and pose pics with, on social networking sites. The increasing sense of desperation over not wanting to be seen as *single*, and therefore, *a loser*, is pushing thousands into grave risks. Some of them date profusely or even marry hurriedly, without checking the credentials of the other and end up hurting themselves terribly.

Do not wish to judge whether it is right or wrong to do it, but have seen couples obsessively seeking a child and spending as many as decades and more in running from pillar to post to make that happen. Alas! A sense of completeness continued to be elusive even after they were blessed with a child. Many such couples can be seen weary and drained out of energy and happiness by the time they get what they were obsessing after.

All of us who think that we shall be happy or at ease or fulfilled after we get this or that, remain largely on the edge always. Either one is at ease or is not; one is contented or is not. Things, people, positions or even fulfilled boons cannot make us happy or contented.

"There are times to stay put, and what you want will come to you, and there are times to get out into the world and find such a thing for yourself."

—Lemony Snicket

Life is a little beyond all that which seems to be...

Let us be true to ourselves. We are not that smart as we would like this world to think. Come on, no one is.

We are pretty naïve, silly and outrightly foolish most of the time. We think we know it all; we think we have all the ingredients and recipes for success, wealth and fame. We think we have it in us to face it all; to take-on what life throws at us! And yet, with the slightest ripple in life, we scamper and scurry, and are at our wits' end. What we seek, we truly do not understand or comprehend in its entirety. What ripples could be unleashed with what we seek, we know not. Hence, let us exercise care and restrain ourselves.

Let us not keep deciding arrogantly as to what we think is the best for us, and then keep ranting or hankering after it obsessively. Yes, of course, all of us would like to be always away from hospitals, police-stations, lawyers and all other unpleasantness in life. All of us would like to live in joy forever. However, to exist in one state of being for one full life-time is just not possible. Whether there is or there is not a higher power, there surely is the principle of *balance* on which our Universe seems to be based. Nature seems to live by the principle of *balance* and moderation. Among all forms of possible life, there are roles and chores divided in balance; there are seasons and eco-systems that maintain balance.

And some kind of a *balance* shall be reflected in our lives too. Yet, there are exceptions to this truth too—for reasons beyond our comprehension. Some people seem to suffer much more and longer than others, and a balance of joy and grief just doesn't come to them. Why, we know not! We need to look closely and ***beyond what seems to be***, even in case of such lives. We can't gauge all truths and all '*plans*' of the higher power...

While giving the final touches to the book, a poem poured out from my heart...

CONTENT

A few crumbs are all I seek
For am a little afraid of 'more'; a little meek!
Not the whole pie it be
No jackpots or bonanzas for me.

Can hold grains of sand not many
Will even a few remain? Not any?
Don't wanna a flock huge
In just a few hearts, I seek refuge.

On a parched heart, few drops of rain
No pennies from heaven; no undue gain
An ounce of clouds merry in the sky
A little will do to wipe off the sigh...

May bring delight the crumbs I seek
May the whole pie not make me go weak
In plenty though make me content
'Aha' may you say at my life spent!

□

Chapter 5

Choosing To Hold On

Had read it somewhere, sometime:

'Life is not what you imagine; it is not even what you wish for...Life is simply what happens with you!' And, particularly so, when we are busy making some plans or trying to arrogantly take charge at the steering wheel!

How true, isn't it?

What is your definition of life?

Millions have tried to define life or to explain it. Varied have been their definitions, perceptions and even their interpretations. And yet, if only they had waited with baited breath for a few more moments. If only they had waited a little to see what happens with them, they would have known: *'errr...well...argghhh... so, this is what life is.'* Each one's definitions would have almost certainly changed, a little or more profoundly. Both, those who declared that *life is a bed of thorns*, or those who found *life beautiful*—would have made some different observations, had they waited for their lives to take another turn, just round the corner.

We do not have to do anything much—other than a bit of efforts though, to live decently; to live well. There is not much need for deep analyses and brainstorming. No matter what you and I think and no matter for how many days and months we think, ultimately *that happens which is to happen.* That is what it is! Not only that is what life is, but that is what decides *who we are*!

Our reactions define us...

Yes, it is our reactions to *what happens*, that define us! Our immediate reaction matters a lot and also our long-term reaction. As there are billions of us inhabiting the planet, so there shall be billions of reactions to incidents of even the same kind. There is no knowing which reaction is correct and which is not. The context matters; the timing and the person matters too. Often, the very same person who reacts with poise and rationale to a grave episode may behave very unreasonably to an insignificant episode, just a few days later. Hence, no point in judging or categorizing people either. No one can be mature and wise all the time, and nor is anyone an impulsive fool at all times in his or her life.

Agreed, that we cannot look at every situation and every conduct of others very sensibly all the time, and that there are bound to be times when we break down or feel despondent or get angry or even become regretful. Some reactions may work on some occasions; others on some other ones. However, it is futile to resolve that we shall look at everything positively all the time. One cannot even be wary and pessimistic all the time.

However, one simple and unassuming reaction that usually works for us all and at all times is: ***to simply hold on***!!! Yes, it works! It works most of the time! Whether as our immediate reaction or our long-term one, it works at all times and in all situations. If only we just wait; we hold on patiently to see what comes next—we would not have to do much *over-thinking* and feel *tense*. Of course, eventually, there might arise a need to think things over and sort out a course of action. At times, one may have to make a decision instantaneously, without ado. Then, one can hold on to whatever follows next.

There are some of us whose first immediate reaction to anything that happens is: *faith and confidence*. However, a few days or weeks later, restlessness and wavering take over...And, in the long run, their reactions largely turn to: *cynicism and whining!* All of this turmoil inside and grappling with one after other thoughts and reactions, can take a toll of one's sanity. Hence, wouldn't it be better if we just wait and watch to begin with? *Hold on to your nerves*; *hold on to your reserves*; and yes, *hold on to the attitude of acceptance* whenever applicable.

If only, we can wait a bit, the unfolding of what comes next can be dealt with, with more clarity.

Do you over-think?

A wise soul did get it right when he or she said:

> "I've got
> 99 problems and 86 of them are
> completely made-up scenarios in my head that I'm
> stressing about for absolutely no logical reason."
> **—Anonymous**

However, we keep thinking; over-thinking about a whole lot of issues and events that haven't even happened as yet. Sometimes, there is one small thing that may have occurred but our response is in much gigantic proportions. We start imagining the worst. It is natural. Yes, it happens to all of us at some point of time or the other. It happens often with me too. Whenever that happens, a dear friend of mine helps me to hold the reins in. However, once the sliding-down commences, it is difficult to stop the boulders from tumbling down on to our gentle mind. We keep sinking then; feeling exhausted and dark and hopeless thereafter.

Even if one isn't in a state or mood to think and sort things out rationally, one can certainly do one act: **JUST WAIT!!!**

Yes, just wait for a night to pass and a day or two to move on...There are bright chances that a new perspective could emerge or that the whole scene changes overnight or several other options emerge. Whatever may be next, but holding on and waiting for a while helps! Osho has written extensively on Heraclitus' belief that *'no man never steps in the same river twice.'* And, it is right, isn't it? Every moment that fleets is followed by a new one. It happens all the time. And newer moments do bring with them new and changing experiences, insights, and thought-processes. It is a matter of just waiting when a moment is dark. The very next one may not be so!

- *When a loved one says a hurting thing or two, we feel as if our world has 'collapsed'. If only we wait for the next morning or even the next week, there could be a sincere apology or a realization or repentance felt by the other. Or, we might look at the whole scene or statement in a completely new light!*

- *If only we just calmly hold on while we wait, in tense anticipation, for the results of pathological tests or for the outcome of an interview or for a publisher to respond after a submission has been sent, our mind and body can be protected from unnecessary harm which we otherwise end up causing!*
- *If only we hold on and wait after a bitter quarrel with a loved one, we might not have to sink to the depths and color the world bitter and dark all around us.*

The clues come...

My personal experiences have always been that whenever I have touched depths, some words have come through a hitherto unexpected source, which have kind of melted the boulders on the chest. Gushing tears staining the cheeks have abruptly stopped and the mist miraculously cleared! Whether by means of a phone call or a video or a song playing on the radio or a sermon or a picture-message or just a casual remark by someone—the light has come! Almost, every time. Hence, the conviction that **not much is as it seems!** One moment, it seemed as though it shall forever be just darkness and the very next moment, it didn't seem so at all.

We need to wait for a bit. A new perspective always emerges; a new light is shed and it all appears different.

Once upon a time, there was this very cute little boy who was the apple of his mother's eye. His mother loved her son beyond measure and pampered him joyously and excessively. Well, he was growing up fine, bit by bit and then the time came for him to be enrolled in a school. The mother found it very hard to part with her darling son even if it was for a few hours, but she had to and she did. She could not bear to see a tear in her loving boy's big round eyes.

One day, the little boy came running into her mother's arms and announced grandly that he was going to be the 'hero' of the school! Nonplussed, the mother asked for details and the panting boy conveyed in broken sentences that there was going to be a play staged in the school on the occasion of the school's Annual Day and that he had 'decided' to be the 'hero' in the play! The mother didn't know how to tell the boy that there would be a selection process and that the chances of he not getting the part were as much as those of he getting it. She was wary of planting any seed of self-doubt in her little boy. Her anxiety heightened each day, as the day of the audition drew near.

Meanwhile, the little boy was full of excitement as he practiced his lines all day long. He didn't know what it meant to 'fail' or to be 'rejected' for a part, and that was his mother's worry. The day of the audition dawned, and all the kids were taken inside the auditorium and the doors were closed. The little boy's mother paced tensely outside all the while.

An hour later, the door opened and the chubby little boy burst out, running and panting and fell in the arms of his mother. The mother anxiously looked at his face to check if he was happy or crying. The boy's eyes were twinkling as he kissed her mom on the cheeks and exclaimed: "Guess what Mom, I've been chosen! Yes, and that too for a very special role! My teacher said: 'You have been selected to clap and cheer'!!!"

Tears of joy streamed down the mother's cheeks as she held her son tight...

It is all about a perspective, isn't it? And a new one emerges from the unlikeliest of corners sometimes! And it comes to us at any age; at any stage in our lives. We need to hold on, however; wait for it to emerge.

All kinds of experiences/people will meet us on the way...

Sometimes, one experiences waves of little and big; beautiful and painful experiences—all in just a single day. Hearts may melt *listening to a domestic-help enthusiastically saving to buy a toy car for her first grandson,* or we may fearfully quiver *reading about an estranged lover who hacked his live-in partner to pieces.*

Some people bring with them their dreariness; others, their sunshine. Some are so nervous that they unnerve us with their weak spirits. Some are brutal, and some narcissistic. And then, sometimes we meet people who *are full of themselves as they sit atop tall towers. They shout and be frantic all the time so as to be heard and seen.* As there are hundreds around us in our circle, so also there are those many vivid experiences.

At times, we find the undeserving ones clutching heaps of laurels that are showered on them, while the meritorious struggle in vain. I often wonder: *When is it harder to hold on? When rejections and failures are thrown at us or when we watch the undeserving folks succeed?*

You must have witnessed your fair share of people and experiences—some intriguing, and others that made you distraught.

One day, in a pensive mood, I asked a friend: *'Is life ever fair?'* He replied: *'Well, whether fair or unfair, it's just there.'*

His reply moved me immensely and a few lines came tumbling out!

It just lies smugly there

Life is beautiful; Life is square
Is it really? Or, is it not?
None can fathom; cringe one may in despair
Perished many, trying to lay it bare!

And, life! Well, it's just there...

We grumble, but we do care
We stumble, but we kind o' fare
We fumble, but we steal our share
Trying to decipher life's why 'n where!

Don't know if beautiful or square
But, life! Well, it's just there...

We toil hard to catch a glimpse
We foil dreams to catch a wink
We recoil in fear, lest we sink
Trying to decipher all of this fun 'n fair!

Don't know if beautiful or square
But, life! Well, it's just there...

What's the purpose; what's the aim?
Are we just pawns in a mere game?
Where are we all headed? It seems in vain...
Trying to, all the while, grimly ensnare!

And, life...? Well, it's just there!

How do you cope?

In any case, I keep my basket full of coping mechanisms handy. I put any one of them to use, depending upon the scene:

- ✓ *Often, I plainly and simply cry.*
- ✓ *At other times, I eat comfort foods or I listen to songs/music.*
- ✓ *I also call and share with one or more dear ones who, I know, shan't judge.*
- ✓ *If no one is around, my books beckon me towards them and provide the much-needed solace.*
- ✓ *Then there are always comedy movies available or romantic-drama series.*
- ✓ *Sometimes, I converse with the One (I believe) who is sitting up there in the sky or has His headquarters on the moon.*

Do you keep a basket handy, for those times when one needs to hold on?

We need a few tools and techniques ready in a basket at all times. Believe me, it is easier then. And, then there is always that one *'best friend'* we all have; that soothes us all and heals all the wounds of all of us. Yes, you are right!

'Time,' it is!!!

Well, it is true that *time* teaches like none other; it heals like none else can, and its most beautiful feature is that it keeps moving...As the times move, everything and everyone changes colors too!

Have been learning from quite a young age onwards—that one must therefore hold on and give *time* to the times that are tough. Ultimately, life moves forward and the tough times do not remain the same.

Everyone has, in his or her heart, a mixed bundle of memories—of good times and bad. And only the one who carries the bundle knows the weight thereof. Sometimes, even when there is no new addition or subtraction in the bundle of memories, it suddenly seems heavier or lighter. Strange, isn't it? Guess, it is the absence or presence of loved ones and good folks around that magically alters the weight of the bundle.

Sometimes, I feel despair carrying my own bundle which magically keeps becoming lighter or heavier at varying times. And, sometimes I feel calm and wise as I look at the contents of the bundle. I do not feel fear in those moments.

Looking around regularly, helps too. One inevitably realizes that there are drearier steps; heavier steps dragging on while struggling to carry their respective bundles. The pain and trauma of some is all too visible, though the real estimate of pain is known to the bearer of the cross!

Do good times teach better or the not-so-good times?

Sometimes, I ask myself: *have the good times been a*

good teacher or the difficult times? There are days when I am able to assert that the difficult times taught some solid lessons! And then there are days when everything is a blur, and I am deeply confused. While lessons were imbedded in both the times, which lessons moved me depended on how wise or foolish; how poor or how generous were my perceptions.

The lessons were equally profound during both the times.

And, during all of the good and bad times, *'people'* played the most crucial role. Be it in crushing feelings or in applying balm over the bruises, there were *'people'* there! Their touch was soothing; they did not have to do anything much. They just egged me to ***hold on***.

When I peep inside my bundle, I can see in hindsight that the bad times weren't *just bad* and the good times weren't *only good*.

What I have understood thus is:

It is not possible to assert as to which kind of times teach better. Lessons are inherent in all the moments. But they are hidden like pearls in the shell. We need to take a ***deep breath***, ***hold on***, and ***look a little inside***. The times when I opened the shell, and took a careful peep inside and allowed myself to learn, I did.

Have you heard of Bethany Hamilton...?

31-year-old Bethany is a professional surfer and writer, based in the United States. Surfing has been a passion of hers since a young age.

She was 13 years old when one day, while surfing with her best friend and a few family members, a tiger shark attacked her. She lost her left arm in the attack. This happened in 2003 at one of the most famous surfing spots in Hawaii. At that age, her dad had been training her to surf and she was just getting popular in the circles. The incident left her bereft of hope. But only for a while...She could have chosen frustration and resignation but she chose tenacity and faith.

One month after the attack, she returned to her board. In fact, in about three months, she entered her first major competition! She got for herself a custom-made board that was longer and slightly thicker than what she had been using and it had a handle for her right arm, thereby making it easier to paddle. She learned to kick more to make up for the loss of her left arm.

Not surprisingly, she is today a name to reckon with among the professional surfers, with lots of awards and championships to her credit. She motivated herself then, and she motivates million others now!

This Universe and its ways are far beyond our wildest comprehensions. Why things happen the way they do and what is the real take, cannot all be fathomed by our severely limited abilities to conceive. All of us have heard or seen or experienced at least a few strange occurrences, which left us perplexed. Can we possibly know or understand millions of such spell-binding occurrences going all around us all the time?

Sometimes, stories are born even before we are born.

In Hillary Clinton's book titled: *Hard Choices*, there is a story mentioned:

The Second World War was going on and a soldier returned home from the front lines for a short break. As he neared the apartment-block where he stayed with his wife, he saw a few men loading a pile of dead bodies on to a truck parked nearby. The man was shocked. A couple of bodies were lying on the road stacked, and about to be loaded on the truck. As the soldier went nearer, he saw a woman's legs in the pile of dead bodies. The woman was wearing shoes, which the soldier identified as his wife's shoes. He demanded to the men who were loading the bodies, that his wife be handed over to him. After an argument, the men gave in and the soldier lifted his wife in his arms and carried her up to their apartment. On examining her, he found that she was still alive! He nursed her back to health.

Eight years later, in 1952, a son was born to them. They named their son Vladimir Putin.

There are stories galore, of people,—not only after they arrived on the planet but even before they came. Strange backgrounds; strange contexts and strange circumstances that have preceded and followed millions of lives.

Yes, millions of us and millions of stories, either awe-inspiring or outrageous. Everyone has heard of how *Oprah Winfrey has dealt with a lot all throughout her life. Her childhood was marked by sexual abuse and all throughout her growing up years she faced issues viz., racism, sexuality, obesity and many more. But she held on and persevered. She worked her way up through the ranks of television, from an anchor at a local network to an international superstar and an unparalleled celebrity, not to mention the fact that she rose to become the richest African-American of the 20th century.*

Yes, hold on!!!

Holding on, is crucial.

At the same time, one ought to also know as to how much to take it.

Outcomes will always be uncertain. Desired results or even slightly positive results may elude even after rigorous struggles. Knowing all of it and yet, choosing to *hold on* and keep going is what remarkable folks are made up of.

Just as J. K. Rowling is.

A few years before she became 'the celebrity' that she today is, she underwent a divorce, and lived on government aid. She could ill-afford to feed her baby and even to have a computer. She manually typed out the 90,000-word novel over and over again so as to send it out to publishers. She did not choose the struggles but she certainly chose to hold on, *even as her first Harry Potter book was rejected by dozens of publishers.*

We cannot comprehend all that which happens every moment. We cannot exactly gauge all the *whys* and *hows* and *why-nots* in this one life-time of ours.

Instead of just breaking our heads and hearts over the unfathomable realities, ***why not just take a deep breath, hold one and wait for the next page to unfold...***

What say...?

□

Chapter 6
Mixed Bags We Are

Nobody is perfect. Nobody can be...It is just not possible. Thousands of years of history which is replete with infinite examples of how everyone of us is a mixed bag, has tried teaching us this glaring truth, and yet we choose to shut our eyes and our heart to this most basic essence of who we are!

We are a sum total of many shades.

The shades are so many that in one life-time we cannot gauge even one person in his or her entirety and at all times. The pit is far too deep. In fact, one life-time isn't enough to fathom oneself. There is no one emotion that governs us all throughout, and there is no one shade that defines us at all times.

We are mixed bags and, on our shoulders, we carry mixed deals!

While we ourselves are an assortment of sorts, the baskets we carry throughout this journey that *life* is, is also full of assorted goodies!

To put it simply: ***'not only are we ourselves mixed bags, but each one has to carry his or her own bundle***

with mixed deals inside, all the while.'

With a mere glimpse of somebody's sunny side, we summarize the whole person thus. But, the very next time as we expect that sunny side to surface, a much darker shade meets the eye and leaves us bewildered. Has this not happened with you too? Just as we expect a particular person to behave in a particular way at a given time, a completely unexpected conduct comes to the fore. When someone who embodied character and depth, emits shallow realities, one wonders if we ever really understood him or her. And when we expect a bleak persona in someone, we are taken aback at the sparkling shimmers we see.

Must have happened with you too, isn't it so? Just as we begin to love and admire a person, a new shade falls over him or her and we recoil. At the same time though, we are not able to let go and reject the person altogether either. Such dilemmas shall always persist because there cannot be straight lines while dealing with people who are alive. Nor is life a straight line. Everything is rigged; blurred and one can never get the shades right. Just as we think we do, a new shade colors the scene in a new light altogether.

Sharanya was about 22-year-old when she fell in love with a colleague of hers at a large investment firm where she had joined barely six months ago. Both were head-over-heels in love with each other. He was four years older to her. They decided it was too early to get married at their age, and hence decided to just go with the flow and enjoy being with each other.

Today, twenty years later, they are still not married.

Sharanya loves Suraj but there are so many starkly contrasting shades that she has seen in him that she is neither able to accept him whole-heartedly and nor, able to break off and live without him. He loves her deeply and unconditionally; is a generous fellow—endearing and a handy-man who has a solution for every issue. However, a few years ago, Sharanya was aghast to discover that he often lied, hid matters from her and engaged in shady financial dealings. On several occasions, she decided to just break up and erase his presence from her life, but they both end up crying every time miserably. Sharanya knows that no one can love her like he does, but at the same time, he is not someone who can be trusted to build a safe haven for a family.

While listening to Sharanya's story, I was reminded of a Professor I knew.

Prof. Moitra was a much-loved Professor in a college in Delhi. Though he taught Chemistry, he was everyone's favorite—across all classes and courses of study in the college. He resembled a typical old grandpa whose cheeks one wished to pull. For students, he was one before whom all the secrets of the heart came tumbling out. He was a friend, mentor, an excellent and intelligent teacher, and a role-model to hundreds of students in the college. Once I happened to meet a friend of his wife. Over the next several meetings, many tales came out in the open about Moitra Sir's life and persona at home. I was stunned to know that the forever-jolly, warm, loving, and generous person whom everyone adored and consulted in all matters, was actually stingy, grumpy, hot-headed and a chauvinist at home!

It was a reminder, despite the jolt. No matter how difficult it is to accept and digest, one has to eventually take in, all shades of a person. A steadfast and helpful friend to everyone outside of home could very well be a disgusting husband and a complete nuisance at home. Actually, if one digs deep into the lives and backgrounds of some of the most loved, adored, and respected people on this planet—be they mentors, philanthropists, teachers, scientists, political leaders, novelists or sport-stars, one is likely to unearth many an unpleasant truth which might make us fling our reverence and beliefs out of the window.

The other day, while listening to *a* program on radio, I was amused to know some facts about a very famous Hindi playback singer of Bollywood. He is a legend and an *institution* by himself. The love, fame, popularity and admiration he amassed in one life, is kind of unparalleled. As his story was being told, my views about him kept swinging like a pendulum. *He was a patriot and on several occasions in his life, he left no one in any doubt regarding that. And yet, he left no stone unturned to avoid paying income-tax, so much so that he often transferred the copyrights of his most famous songs to his secretary! He was very friendly, jovial, and easy-going but at the same time, he was a shrewd miser.*

A listener like me would assume that if he was a miser and avoided tax, he would never sing for anyone for nothing. And yet, the pendulum swung again.

There were two very famous personalities: one, an actor and the other, a revered director, from both of whom this singer never charged money for singing. And yet, this very same person never sang/recorded for anyone until the full payment due to him was made in advance. His secretary would give him the signal that payment was received and then he would come to the mic and sing. Furthermore, he had a great sense of humor but was also known to be moody and grim at times.

At the end of the show, I was non-plussed. I didn't know whether to like him and merrily sing his songs as always or whether to remember the other shades of this person and never idolize him again?

As long as we do not have to live with certain folks, the fact that they are mixed bags doesn't affect us very much. For that matter, every single person has varied shades and angles, be he or she a celebrity or a lay-person. It is only when we discover certain truths about people amongst whom we must live, that we need to make up our mind and choose what to do.

Can we change people?

Many wise souls advise us that *we must accept people (particularly those whom we like or love) as they are, and not try change them.*

The fact is *we cannot change anybody.*

Wisdom lies in *never trying to change anybody.*

Sensibility lies in *not assuming that we have the power to change anybody.*

Sensitivity and grace lie in *never thinking that anybody needs to be changed!*

We are wasting our time and effort and ushering anguish in our lives, if we think and attempt otherwise. Nobody has been able to change anybody. Of course, the little molding and nurturing that happens in childhood does alter certain intrinsic ways of ours.

It is nearly impossible to change people, but there are two ways in which change can still occur in the whole bargain. ***How*, you may ask.** Well, in two ways precisely:

✓ *...if a situation changes the other person. Situations have the potency to change folks—for good or for worse. Actually, this difference is also incomprehensible most of the times!*

Or,

✓ *...if a situation changes our perception towards that person, or towards everyone and towards life itself!*

Without one of the above two events happening, nothing changes.

Here is a true story/episode in the life of a friend's friend, (albeit the names are changed) which I had penned for my blog, a while ago:

30-year-old Aryan did not like to be at home. In fact, he did not like his family members much. Not that there were too many of them, but he felt that they were so very unproductive. They sat at home just doing nothing, while he was already climbing the socio-economic ladder and taking rapid strides as the deputy general manager in an advertising agency.

Aryan was particularly irritated at his 25-year-old younger brother Tejas who lacked ambitions or even a vision. He had graduated nearly three years ago, but was still confused as to what to do ahead. He had made it repeatedly clear all this while that he would not apply for just about any job that others found suitable for him.

He often yelled whenever a murmur arose at home over he doing nothing. Aryan and Tejas would end up quarrelling bitterly more than once in a week, as each accused the other of not understanding his perspective.

The ageing parents sat looking helplessly at their two sons, who had grown so apart; so very unable to tolerate each other for a minute. Aryan had made it clear that he would marry only after he had his own apartment and set-up. The bitterness was aggravated by the fact that he alone had to shoulder all responsibilities at home, and this slowed down his upbeat plans to buy an apartment for himself.

One fine Sunday, Tejas left home early in the morning so as not to have any verbal duels at home with Aryan. Just the previous night, they had fought over what to watch on Netflix. Aryan had ended up saying some hurtful words to his younger brother.

Aryan woke up late and found his mother bottling up mango pickle which she had been keenly making over the week. He brusquely enquired after his breakfast and on finding his father watching an acrimonious debate on a news channel, told his mother to get his breakfast in his room itself. Aryan could never understand his own Appa and that how and why could he just take quite an early voluntary retirement and not do anything worthwhile the whole day. It seemed as if all three of them had shrugged off all worries from the day he had taken up his first job. He did not like it one bit that they sat helplessly looking up at him for meeting their needs.

"Aryan, here—have upma and a half-boiled egg as you like it. Shall I make tea or coffee with it?" Amma asked as

she entered Aryan's room holding the tray in her hands.

"Will have black tea," Aryan replied curtly. "Where is your pampered one?" he asked.

Amma sheepishly replied: "He got up quite early and left without having anything. Didn't say where he was going." He grunted as he digged into the egg.

Amma was still standing.

"Well, what....?" Aryan asked impatiently.

"Was errrrrr, wondering if you have ten minutes to spare?" Amma's tone was hesitant and soft.

"What is it? Do not tell me to go out on a Sunday to buy the grocery. Please! Have told you umpteen times. Tell Tejas to...."

"No...No...it is not that," Amma interrupted. "Wanted to send across a bottle of our mango pickle to Savita's place. I had promised her last week and she must be waiting for it," Amma said it in one breath.

"I do not know any of your friends or where they stay, Amma! Please do not keep such weird chores for me to do on the only day off that I get after a week," Aryan snapped.

Following a few tears in Amma's eyes, a few muffled sobs and a cup of tea, Aryan was on his way to Savita Aunt's house—about 4kms away. The address and Amma's directions were thankfully straightforward. He reached the flat and rang the bell. A lady in her late 50s opened the door, while wiping her hands off a napkin she was clutching in her hands. Aryan managed to smile and briefly mutter a few words introducing himself and extended the bag with the bottle of pickle towards her. Savita Aunty, delighted to see her friend's handsome son, held his hand and pulled him inside the house. The next instant she disappeared inside, while mentioning something about seating comfortably and a hot cup of tea.

Aryan was eager to leave and return home and catch up with his buddies. Less than 5 minutes later, Savita Aunty was back, bringing with her a cup of tea and a plate of piping hot dal-vadas. The aroma of vadas filled up the room and Aryan could not hold himself back. Savita Aunty kept chatting amicably and asking him questions about his job, plans to marry and so on...

Another 5 minutes and Aryan got up to leave. He thanked her and walked towards the door to step out. As he did so, he happened to glance towards a door on his left to what would have been the bedroom. The door was partially ajar and Aryan could catch just a glimpse of a single bed on which someone was lying down. He stepped outside, and bowed to touch Savita Aunt's feet, bid goodbye and took the stairs.

"Amma, who else lives along with Savita Aunty in her house?" Aryan asked on reaching home.

"Aha, you met her son and his dog?" Amma was excited. "I have never met them myself, till now."

"No, I did not meet anyone...and what are you saying? Was there a dog too? Well, neither of them came out while I was there and if I had done that, you would have lectured me about manners and courtesies etc.", Aryan snapped.

Amma's tone became pensive all of a sudden. Tears welled up in her eyes for the second time that day. "Savita's son is a child with special-needs. He can walk around but he does not speak or even understand much. I do not know the details exactly but he is challenged in many ways. He has no friends. He never speaks with anyone. Many years ago, a relative brought a dog for him to keep him company. Well, the dog is his only friend and companion ever since. Around twilight, he steps out of the house with his dog and they slowly take a walk around the building and return home. They have been doing this ritual since the time the dog has come home. Otherwise, the son keeps lying down in the bedroom and the dog silently sits down next to the bed."

"But Amma, why did he not even bark when I rang the bell or went inside," asked Aryan in an emotionally-laden voice.

"Savita says that the dog is so attached with the boy that it does not move at all anywhere without him. Even when a visitor comes home, the dog is not curious to know who has come, for he never leaves the boy alone for an instant. Moreover, since the boy is sleeping most of the time, this dog does not even bark, lest the master would be disturbed."

An awkward silence ensued...

"Oh, I think your Appa is calling..." Amma could not hold back her tears and rushed towards the kitchen.

Aryan stood standing there in the living room near the shoe-cabinet. He walked slowly towards the balcony and sat down there on a high stool. A lot of thoughts were scrambling inside for space: 'When the dog would have come to their house, he would have expected the little boy to play and have fun with him. But how much time he would have taken to understand that my master has special needs; that he has challenges...? How exactly would the dog have altered its own basic nature and instincts to adapt himself to the boy's needs? How must the dog have understood what to do so as to win his master's trust and become his best friend...? Just by observing mutely?'

Aryan kept looking out at the huge trees lined up outside in the lane. Children were playing under a few trees while a few weary ones were resting underneath. The trees did not seem to mind. They just stood there majestically and who was the beneficiary of their shade did not matter to them one bit. 'Just like the dog...Whether the master was wealthy or healthy or challenged did not matter one bit to the dog. He simply knew that he had to be his master's best friend.'

The door-bell rang and he came out of his reverie. He got up to open the door. Tejas was standing outside. Without meeting his elder brother's gaze, he came inside.

Aryan smiled. He was feeling light—as if something was taken off from his shoulders.

"Amma, is lunch ready? Tejas is home too. Let us all eat together today. And, I want to taste the pickle too."

A sudden turn-of-events, or even a minor nudge sometimes can alter our perceptions or others' conduct.

Well then, the next inevitable question that pops up is:

Is it possible to accept folks as they are?

My experience says that not many of us can accept any other in honest totality and with no reservations. Well, if by '*acceptance*,' we mean living with a person or spending a life-time together or even loving a person—then, yes, we can! With little or more compromise though! We do like and live with many people all the time, but with each one—there is some or the other pang; a little hurt sometimes; a little let-down at times; or a little disappointment. The scene is quite sad for those who have no escape; for those who have to helplessly live with one or more *unacceptable* people in their lives.

Sometimes, there is a dull nagging pain that lurks somewhere all the time, when we live with people we don't very much wish to. Surely, some or the other trait of every person *disappoints*. We all have to accept a little hurtful word or conduct of one or many all the time. Often, that one hurtful thing isn't there all the time but surfaces once in a while, and particularly, when least expected. However, we try to ignore or just convince ourselves and continue.

What have been your experiences?

Have you seen or experienced relationships wherein all is smooth and there are no mixed deals?

Even when two sisters or two best friends love each other most dearly, there are moments when some thing or the other surfaces which *hurts*. We *accept* others, but not without shedding tears at times or feeling hurt once in a while. To be wholly understood by someone and be wholly loved too; just unconditionally and totally will be nothing short of a miracle. It just does not happen. A little spice; a little off-beat shade or two and/or a little irritation occasionally will be there.

What to do?

This is one question we have heard popping up from inside us the greatest number of times. ***What to do?*** Other than in the case of a few frivolous affairs of the heart, we cannot reject or do without people whom life drops in our laps.

A SIMPLE WORKABLE SOLUTION I can think of is:

✓ *To go on with those who are irreplaceable. About them—accept what you can and even what is not easy to. A few tears can be shed once in a while, but the ties can be preserved if they are really worthwhile. After all, there is no one who isn't a mixed bag.*

✓ *And, whenever possible—to remove oneself from the scene; from the precincts of people who are hurting us. Identify those who are taking a toll of our physical, mental and emotional health, and shrug them off.*

However,

- Wisdom *lies in knowing who is in category 1 and who is in category 2; and in knowing that there are some who transcend all categories.*
- Wisdom *lies in knowing oneself; in knowing when someone's hurtful behavior starts hurting you and to stop just before that happens.*
- Wisdom *lies in knowing, based on your own true nature, what is acceptable to you and what isn't.*

Keeping in view my very limited capabilities to take shallow conduct in people, I too have removed myself from many lives. I did not accept them as they were. Don't know if I missed anything in the process, but I did what felt peaceful. I did not do it at one stroke, or after one hurtful experience. I did try to look *beyond what was very obvious.* I tried to *let-go*; to give more and expect less, but I recognized there were a couple of ties which just could not be resuscitated.

However, I do wish them well, always!

Have you had such ties, which eventually wilted away? Have you ever distanced yourself from some people, while accepting a few others with all their shades?

Hold on to the precious mixed-bags

A plane crash survivor recounted the three lessons he learnt in the experience of surviving the crash. He could have died as the others did in the crash. However, he lived, and learnt a lesson or two. He said:

'It all changes in an instant. We have this bucket list; list of people we plan to visit or talk to but I just learnt in a flash that moment that never ever to postpone anything.

I thought in that instant: I've lived a good life. I've tried to get better at everything I've tried. But I had also allowed my ego to matter. I regretted all the moments spent on things that did not really matter—with people who mattered. I thought of my relationships with my wife, my friends and as I reflected, I decided to eliminate negative energy from my life. I am not perfect right now and nor is life but it's a lot better. I no longer try to be right; I choose to be happy.

The third lesson I learnt as the plane was coming down and the pilot was trying to land on water was that dying is not scary. But I didn't want to go. And yet, we keep preparing for death for as long as we live. I only wished that if I could see my kids grow up'.

The one line which touched the most was: 'I regretted all the moments spent on things that did not really matter—with people who mattered.'

While all of us are mixed-bags, at least a few need to be accepted as they are. Ironically, we spend a lifetime trying to change dozens of them; trying to win the affection of dozens or even hundreds of them; trying to make everyone happy; trying to like and be liked by everyone and then expecting them to equally reciprocate. All this stress n strain is usually followed by hurt and gloom. And then, the journey gets over; life is finished, while we are still bitter, hurt, and discontented.

And all we had to do was to channelize our wisdom and energies towards identifying some five or six precious relationships, and then *accepting them no matter how mixed a deal they were...*

□

Chapter 7

Observe Reactions!

There was a time our observation skills were quite sharp. We could keenly observe and gauge even that which was not apparently noticeable.

When???

Yes, you guessed it right!

We could do that when our minds were not so very mechanically wired as they are now; when we had few distractions on our minds, and fewer distractions in our hands! Children were believed to be wiser than adults, as they could observe intently and therefore, learn better. Their insights were sharper because their observations were astute. They could see all that which we failed to.

There is that fairly well-known story of *a little girl who was one day sitting at one of the back benches in the school and intently drawing something. The little girl usually remained distracted in most of the classes. She never sat straight or intently focused whenever any other subject was being taught. Noticing her deep concentration while drawing, the teacher went up to her and asked: "What are you drawing?" The girl looked up, smiled sweetly and replied: "I am drawing a picture of*

God". The teacher was intrigued. She asked: "Well, no one has seen God. Nobody knows what God looks like." The little girl's big wide eyes shone brightly as she said: "Well, now they will, in a minute."

Kids can often see what we simply can't. Even if they are wrong, they take a chance. They keenly notice all that there is around them, and sometimes—even what is not very obvious.

Had we not squandered off all their talents and abilities by bombarding them with gadgets so that we could please them and remain elevated in their eyes, they could have dazzled and shone beyond our estimate. However, not many innocent eyes sparkle these days or open widely as an idea descends in them.

Alas! Those times have passed. Our minds are crammed these days with the worst junk possible and our hands are forever clicking and swirling mechanically on screens. Heads are bent; and eyes are downcast. How can one observe keenly then? ***To look at the obvious, one needs to carefully observe, and to look at what lies beyond the obvious, one needs to very keenly observe.***

How will *Observing* help us?

How sensible are our own reactions, do depend on how well we observe the actions of others. If we observe well, and not deduce a heapful after just a glance; not jump to conclusions about people, events and circumstances, a welcome change in our lives can very well be ushered. Sound and steady observations have the power to astound us!

Had once read somewhere: *'Pay attention. It's all about paying attention. Attention is vitality. It connects you with others. It makes you eager. Stay eager.'*

One can start by observing every*thing* around us! *Whether a swinging branch or shape of a leaf or how a cat leaps or how a bird looks intently at the surroundings—* there is so much to observe. And once we get into the habit of observing, everything seems so very fascinating. Even *a crack on a wall and the steady marching of ants is so very intriguing.*

Observe and ponder over everything possible...

Either we will learn or we will just feel joy.

Observe *a pencil or an eraser closely; stare intently at a ceiling fan or the froth that waves bring to the shore; at mosses & lichens growing on fallen logs. Just notice how fungi grow on the trees; how the stripes of sunlight stream through the curtains and cast a halo on your favorite chair and how the steam swirls up from your morning cup of coffee.*

And then, gradually the streak of observing seeps deeper inside us. And along with observing *things,* we begin to observe people and events that happen with us, equally intently. Further, as we begin to decipher all the whys, *hows,* and *whats* more carefully, we might feel as if huge boulders are lifted off our shoulders. Our reactions to actions of others, will then largely be one of amusement. Fewer people and happenings will trouble or stir the mind.

The precious time that we spend wondering why things and folks do not turn out as they should have or as we expected them to, will instead be filled with interesting lessons and joys that you have deduced by observing the *obvious* and the *not-so-obvious*.

How well we comprehend depends on how well we observe!

Those who observe keenly, do comprehend intelligently. Most of us have read one such story of Birbal in our childhood.

Once Birbal was sent to another kingdom as an ambassador. The King, of that kingdom, had heard a lot of stories about Birbal's sharp intellect and thought of testing the same. The King made all his ministers dress up like him, and thereafter, they all sat in a line to test Birbal's intelligence. When Birbal entered the courtroom to offer his credentials, he was amazed to see everyone dressed in the same clothes and sitting on a similar kind of throne.

Perplexed, Birbal took a moment to observe everyone very keenly, and then went up to one of them and bowed in front of him. It was the King himself, who was surprised beyond words. He stood up and hugged Birbal and asked him how could he guess so? Birbal smiled and answered: "My lord, you exuded sparkling confidence which no one else did. And not only that the rest of them even kept looking at you for approval. And that gave me the clue that you indeed are the king." The King felt amused and praised Birbal for his unmatched intellect and presence of mind.

A little similar to the above story is a modern day one:

A father had a very close bond with his only son and they were very good friends to each other. The son went abroad for his higher studies and visited his father during the breaks. Just before the son's final semester was to get over and he was to return home, he shared with his father that he was in love with a girl in his class and that she too belonged to the same city where they lived. The father was super excited and teased his son even as the son could not stop blushing on the video call. When the father pressed for details, the son challenged his father with a bet.

The father was all game for it. The son said: "Dad, you say that you are very smart and that you can read people by observing their faces. Well, I challenge you now. She will be on the same flight as I will be boarding. Amongst hundreds of people who shall come out of the Arrivals gate at the airport, let me see if you can spot my chosen one. I shall offer no clue to you. However, I will tell you this that I shall come out about 15 minutes after her." The father burst out laughing and accepted the son's challenge wholeheartedly.

On the said day and time, the father stood at the Arrivals gate, and kept recording on video cam the movement of hundreds of people as they came outside. After recording for about 30-40 minutes, his adorable son finally came out of the terminal and both the buddies joyously hugged each other tight. The father told his son: "Hey, champ! You have given me two hours to figure out the girl you love, from amongst the hundreds who came out today from the gate. Well, I think I already know. But, let us reach home and let me double-check my recording. Meanwhile—you freshen up and then be ready to part with the Rs 10,000/- that you will have to pay me, as was agreed." The son shook his head in disbelief and they teased each other all the way home.

A few hours later, the father told his son to come to his room. The son excitedly raced to his father's room and there on the big TV screen, was the still image of the girl he loved. He was dumbstruck, and a look of adoration shone on his face as he hugged his father lovingly. "But... but...how could you? There were so many girls coming out of the gate. How could you figure out?", stammered the son.

The father laughed, winked and with a twinkle in his eyes, replied: "Well, son—you see when people who live abroad return home, they are very excited to come out of the gate and embrace their loved ones. Everybody's eyes keep searching longingly for familiar faces waiting outside to receive them. No one looks back. Well, this girl—when she was coming out with her trolley, she twice looked back. Her eyes were probably searching for you, since you were going to come out after her. I checked the recording again at home, and I knew it for sure then. And, of course, there was this glow all about her which only those who are in love, have!"

Do you jump to conclusions?

It happens with us all the time. People often say things to throw us off-guard or to deceive us. If only we observe carefully, we would know that the words are just not true; they were uttered to make us believe something which was not the truth. Even as people speak, observe them keenly. More than half of the spoken words are never really meant. And, silly we! We keep building and breaking ties, based on what we just see or hear, at the superfluous level. Do refrain from being presumptuous.

Please do not jump to conclusions at the drop of a hat. There are hidden feelings; hidden messages; not-so-apparent traits and thoughts behind what people say and do. Just take a pause. *Look beyond...*

This habit of jumping to conclusions can hit us hard. We *look and hear*, whereas we ought to *observe and listen*. Aaaahh! One is likely to miss so many moments; miss out some amazing feelings, facts and folks altogether if we do not try and take a peep *beyond what seems to be.*

There is this incredible story of an incredible man I read about:

An old man in his 90s lives in an ordinary rental apartment in the city of San Francisco. At first sight, you or I would just brush past him and not look twice if we happened to bump into him anywhere. His clothes are just ordinary and glasses, simple and old. He does not carry an expensive bag or wear a costly watch. There is no 'brand' one can see on him. A couple of years ago, one could have bumped into him in a bus, for he does not own a car. However, we would not have cast another look at him or tried to observe him closely, for he is not a famous actor or politician or a star in any field.

But hey, a star indeed he is! Not in a field we commonly know of, but he is one of the few brightest beacons in the sea of humanity.

He is Chuck Feeney.

He has donated $8 billion to charitable causes. He can best be described as: 'someone frugal with himself but generous with others.' He likes to and he has made money, but unlike the millions of rich people around, he does not like to spend it on himself.

He believes in 'giving while living'!!! He has contributed $588 million to Cornell University, $125 million to University of California and $60 million to Stanford University. Outside of the US, he has spent $1 billion to renovating/building Universities in Ireland. He has spent millions on modernizing Vietnam's health-care system; millions on turning New York's neglected Roosevelt Island into a technology hub and spent generously on many many life-changing ventures. He thinks and lives like a monk. His take on charity is: 'since you can't take it with you, why not give it all away and have control of where it goes and see the results with your own eyes.'

He is not interested in fame and makes his donations anonymously. Hence, he is not famous. We would not think much of him, if we were to accidentally meet him. But if only, we take a pause with people; if only we talk, we observe and if only we scratch the surface, several gems would shine brilliantly and flood our hearts with wonder.

What next after *observing*?

Well, what to do after we have peered intently and observed patiently? How does all of it or any of it, make any difference to us?

It does...

Yes, it greatly impacts our well-being; our state of mind and our overall character. We do not get upset too soon and on too many things because we see people and developments more clearly. That completely changes our outlook towards everything that happens in life. When someone says something offensive or acts contrary to our expectations—we observe the words or the acts keenly; muse over them; and try to see the overall context in which something was said or an act was done. Once *keen observation* becomes a habit, we could either understand people better or we could become further miserable because the weaknesses of others might become too visible! Although observing has to be cultivated as a habit, what we observe is our choice.

After a spell of observing keenly, the following attitudes must follow:

Either we just ACCEPT people as they are, very gracefully

OR

We keep an eye on the OVERVIEW and/or the CONTEXT in which people behave the way they do and try to see what is not always visibly apparent

The two years (when the covid-19 pandemic struck) of staying aloof, socially-distant and un-connected with the outside world—gave me one gift, though. I got a glimpse of *the key*.

Irritants, issues, dilemmas, hurtful moments, plans going awry—and many more such episodes will always be sprinkled on the path where we tread. The key lies in how well do we *Observe, Accept and Flow*.

There is just no need to decide most of times; and we needlessly break our heads and lose our calm. A much saner option is to calmly receive, observe what we have received, accept it and flow with the tide. I know this sounds cliché but this is it! Till that moment hits us individually, we may brush it aside as cliché, but when it hits, it sinks...

On looking back, I too feel abashed at the declarations I often made with pride or at the times I swore to staying out of or in so many lives or at the grand plans I harbored for myself and others. Of course, it is not that one cannot or ought not to do anything at all, but most of what we decide or think for the larger part of our lives, amounts to nothing. A few baby-steps or tactical plans for the ongoing day or the next day are fine, but sensibility calls for spending the precious hours of life in training the mind to observe, *accept* and *flow*.

Accept and flow...

Once we accept a way of life or a way of thinking—it does not certainly mean that we obsess or fret over it all the time and build up stress inside while trying to hold on to these ways. It also does not mean that we cease observing further. Keep noticing the big and small things and keep learning, accepting and flowing too.

Do not forget to remind yourself now and then:

What I believe in, today, may also not be the ultimate truth. I accept this calmly too, today. Nothing can ever be said with certainty and nothing can ever be labeled with confidence as ***the right*** *or* ***the wrong****. It is best to remain in a state of flow and flux.*

As it comes, so it shall be...

As it seems, so is one to accept...

I do not know for how many days shall I remember all of this or how successfully shall I train my mind accordingly, but to stumble and fall; to feel silly and ashamed; or to allow life to spank hard once in a while—

is also **acceptable** and I shall **flow** with all of it.

I often myself go back to my sources of inspiration and either re-read a few lines which had transformed life once or peer over a particular para in a book which had become the turning point once or listen again to a *ghazal* that always stirs me deeply within...It is alright to forget all the lessons and resolutions after a while or to go back to old ways or to break the decisions we make. Is it not?

This trait can seep inside us much better if we allow others to do the same. Those who observe others intently, and yet remain amused; not judgmental, can observe their own selves much better. They can 'pause' better; learn better and though sensitive, they can remain largely unruffled.

Each one of us is a mixed bag and then our lives, are further mixed, complicated and multi-faceted that it is absolutely no sense in labeling or judging. While observing others at all times is good, the lessons are interesting when we observe those who are in love. Our conduct becomes so very intriguing and even, incredible, isn't it, when we are in love...?

Maya was a housemaid from Nepal, working in Doha, Qatar for a prosperous native Qatari family. Shadaab was a technician from Pakistan and worked for a private construction firm in Qatar.

She was a dark, short young girl—very warm and loving. He was a generous, though a little short-tempered young man.

During those days, Shadaab was deployed as the Supervisor on a road construction project and for a week, work had been going on just outside the Qatari villa where Maya was employed. Every day, Maya regularly came outside in the mid-afternoon to offer water, tea etc. to the workers working on the road. Her *Madam* had instructed her to do that work of *Sabab*[*].

After about a week since Maya came out every afternoon with the beverages, they cast a serious look at each other and very soon, they were exchanging flirtatious smiles. The work on that stretch of the road was completed in a month's time. They were in love, by then. They had spoken to each other on several occasions during the tea-breaks and shared their details of family, work, and life in Doha. She was a Christian and was unmarried. Maya had lost both her parents at an early age, and following her other siblings she had landed in the Gulf nation to do menial jobs from a tender age. She had attended school for just five years, before being transported to Qatar. He was a Muslim and had a family in Pakistan—with a wife, three children and parents.

Shadaab loved his wife and children but had not met them since four years. He felt lonely most of the times and struggled to sustain himself in the strange land.

---

* *Sabab*: for a good cause

Not many could understand their kind of *love*? Was it merely a set of *needs* manifesting as love? Life as an expatriate, particularly when one is at the lowest rung of the social ladder, is not easy. There is a whole range of physical, security, financial, mental and emotional issues that one finds oneself persistently grappling with. It is but so very natural to seek solace, companionship and convenience. Thousands of miles away from the comfort of one's own world, men seek the convenience of company and home-cooked food; while women seek companionship and security. And, of course, who would not be happier with a little care and affection too. Those few, who came to know of their affair, reacted differently. Some expressed outrage; while some others thought it was a *silly* temporary affair, nothing more than a bubble. For most, it was just yet another mutually convenient arrangement meant to last till either did not go back home, for good.

Maya's *Madam* adopted a patronising attitude and decided to bless the affair. Maya and Shadaab were both married in Qatar in the presence of two witnesses.. She was twenty one years old when her marriage took place with Shadaab. Despite the hard work, she had not yet lost the *spark*; the *mischief* and the *twinkle* in her eyes. With Shadaab in her life, all the struggles and hard work seemed further worthwhile.

They rented a very small *mulhaq* (outhouse) for themselves and though she was legally required to stay in the house of the Qatari household, her *Madam* had allowed her to complete her work and leave by late evening and report early next day.

Although Shadaab could not let anyone in his country know of this second marriage, he had decided to give his best to it and take good care of Maya for as long as they were going to be together in Qatar. He had a generous heart that was sensitive to everyone's needs and concerns. She maintained her faith, despite the technicalities on paper, and continued her Friday visits to the Church.

Both did not know what future held for them. She could not take a husband from a different religious faith to her own folks in Nepal. And he too could not let his family or friends know of this marriage. They decided to *love* and *live*, in and for the present. While she cooked delicacies for him, he shopped for her and brought her little trinkets, clips, and many other *things*. Over their meals, they both spent hours sharing their dreams and fears; joys and little troubles.

Years flew by, and they lived happily together...

Twenty years have passed since Shadaab and Maya had entered into wedlock. Maya has taken up a part-time job with another Indian family residing in Doha. She continues to take care of her *Madam*'s family though after her *Madam*'s death a year ago, the grown-up children do not need her for the entire day.

At the end of the first week with the Indian family, her new *Madam* asked her: "Maya, are you married?"

"Yes *Madam*," Maya replied softly, after a brief pause.

"And kids?"

"No *Madam*, no kids".

"Did you get married here, after coming to Doha or he came with you from Nepal?"

Maya smiled shyly. "*Madam*, he is from Pakistan and we met here".

Maya's *Madam* shot a quizzical expression at her, obviously not expecting such an alliance between two nationalities.

"What are you saying? Really...?"

"Yes, *Madam*..."Maya replied with an amused look on her face.

"Is he good?" Maya's new *Madam* was concerned.

"Yes *Madam*, very much so... He is very good and is unlike other men".

"Does he take good care of you?"

"Yes, *Madam*... He does".

Maya's *Madam* recollected all of a sudden that Maya got a call every day in the morning at 9 am, and she assured the caller every day that she was fine and had eaten her breakfast. Must be him-- *Madam* told herself.

She asked Maya: "How many years now since your marriage?"

"Twenty years, *Madam*".

"But then, what is your future? Will you go to Pakistan? Or will he come with you to settle in Nepal? After all, we cannot stay here in Qatar permanently".

"*Madam*, I cannot go to Pakistan because he has a complete family there."

"Then, will he simply leave you and forget you one day?"

"It will not be fair... Why should he leave his children and wife? Only to be with me? But they were there in his life before me and they are dependent on him".

"Well, don't you have a problem with this? Once he goes there, he is not going to remember you. You will regret it when he will finally leave you and go to stay with his wife?'

"No, *Madam*. She is also a woman, and a good woman. She too cares deeply for him." After a moment's hesitation, Maya continued: "*Madam*, it has been three years since he has left Qatar. He now lives in Pakistan. He lost his job and could not stay on".

"Oh! God! He has already left you? What will you do in your old age? How are you going to manage it all by yourself?"

"What to do, *Madam*? He had to leave and we always knew this separation was going to happen. He still calls every day, and cares. He panics every time there is a dust-storm here or there is any other security threat that he comes to know of."

She paused for a moment and wiped the tears welled up in her eyes. And then with a smile on her tired face, she continued: "I was happy for seventeen years... We married for the present, not the future. God is kind! He brought in my life a caring person. I lived happily. And *Madam*, life is like that only..."

Bruce Lee observed water and it taught him lessons which no person or philosophy could not teach him.

Maya's Madam in the above story, got quite a remarkable lesson in love, from her domestic help.

Beginning with the inhaling and exhaling of our breath, which can teach us some amazing lessons and truths of life, everything, every moment and every person carries infinite potential to impart wisdom and make an impact. We just need to be aware; we need to be ready!

Are you...?

□

Chapter 8

Some Squares Shall Be Always Empty...

Have seen so many folks all around me trying to have it all, but it is always in vain. Many a times, my own heart has childishly yearned for this and that, and all of everything in life, but it is indeed always in vain!

None can have it all.

Do you have everything?

Do you have a perfectly satisfactory job/profession; a perfect life-partner and a wonderful life complete with the best of things, friends, journeys, health and contentment?

Is your life complete? Do you have 'everything' that you think you should?

If your answer is 'no,' then you are very normal and one amongst the billions of us. However, if your answer is 'yes', your life is one rare exception. Or, probably, you think you have everything that you need, but you yourself do not correctly know as to what is it you truly need! Or, perhaps, as per the yardstick of the world, there are still a few squares that are empty?

A couple of months ago, had mused and penned:

The empty squares

Life is a crossword puzzle—unique.
Picking up the clues, each must
Chalk out the path to take
And search for answers his own.

Working up one's way through
Sometimes erring;
Often rejoicing on hitting it right
Fill up the squares; weaving a pattern harmonious.

Not all squares get to be filled up though;
Empty squares come for all; we must live with ours
Some have love missing; others an organ of the body
Some wealth...others find simple tasks challenging
Sadly, in some—a heart or its beat missing...

Some do not mind music in their lives amiss
Others insist on a melody of their own...
Some live happily despite balance missing in the bank
Others live uneasy till the former is traded, with the latter.

In the horde to fill up squares optimum;
Cleverly we calculate
Alas! But the squares which came full get empty
Our bids continue unabated though
Bargains we ceaselessly make.

Hard we strive to fill up all the squares
Often through means questionable;

Some others still fall empty
And the incompleteness haunts.

Gazing at the final picture; the net gain
Remorse fills up
Wish the puzzle was enjoyed unsolved;
With the few empty squares as came with life itself.

Yes, let us assume for a moment that life is a big board-game like chess, on which there are squares. On everybody's board, there are some squares that are full and some which are blank or empty. The irony of life is that, if you desperately seek to fill up one empty square, some other square usually becomes empty. The message, as I have understood over the years, is that: **no one can have it all!**

No one that I know of, has *everything* in life. Do you? Sometimes, there are people who have all that they need or all that is crucial to a good life, but they lack *awareness* of it and this again means that they lack something very significant, which is *'consciousness.'* They remain oblivious to the vastness of all they have been endowed with, and thus automatically, the square of '*gratitude*' is therefore empty. And if this crucial square is empty, the other full ones too shall not mean much. There will be a sense of void or emptiness tugging all the while...

Should we then, therefore, not try to *Achieve* what we don't have?

Of course, you must!

There is one minor difference though between trying to achieve and obsessing over having something; between striving towards a goal steadfastly and going crazy in order to amass it all. Trying to achieve a goal is different from desperately hankering after something! The difference is minor, so much so that the seeker himself or herself does not sometimes realize as to when a *struggle* or a *striving* becomes an *obsession* or a *desperation*. The threshold may be a thin line but the outcomes are poles apart.

In lives all around us and in fact, even in our own life—a simple glance all around shall suffice.

Someone has good looks but good health is elusive; someone has all the money but not an iota of warmth and love; someone has the ambition but not one opportunity; and someone has a loving family but the square of self-actualization is blank. Similarly, someone can afford to travel the whole world over dozens of times, but there is no compatible companion to go with, while there are those who have a loved one but cannot afford a single trip. Someone has a life-partner but no love in life; while someone is blessed with love, but a seal of permanence is amiss.

Looking at umpteen lives around me, I feel that yes, some squares shall always be empty and unless the needs are pressing or the situation is dire, one must largely leave life at that. We must accept the emptiness in a few squares gracefully, while being ever grateful for the squares that aren't empty. Of course, if there is not food on the table or if health is deteriorating, efforts must be directed towards restoring good health and procuring sufficient food.

Everybody needs a nudge though, and regularly too!

Yesterday, I found in my inbox yet another mail of rejection sent by a publisher. There it was—sitting and mocking at me.

Over the past three decades or so, I have lost the count of the number of messages or calls or e-mails that have been hurled at me—all saying that my job applications or my articles or my proposals of a book or my bid at scholarships or my papers for presentation or my dreams of making it at the civil services' exam, are rejected.

And surprisingly, it hurts the same, every time. Whether one is 15 or is 50, when a dream or a passion is roughly tossed aside or brutally flung at a wall—it hurts. Guess, one just never gets really used to dejection.

Before I could slip further low into self-pity, I reminded myself that the square of ***'ability to express myself'*** *is full and brimming in my life! A person could be born into a publisher's family but if he or she has this square empty, the opportunities which come with birth in such a family amount to nothing! I reminded myself, that about 40-50 steady friends of mine sincerely read whatever I write. So, the square of* ***'being read and appreciated'*** *is not all that empty either.*

On other occasions when dejection overwhelms me, a spark emerges from nowhere which reiterates that it is good that certain squares are empty and thankfully, the most crucial ones are not. As long as there is a roof on one's head and food on the plate, and good health to be able to eat that food, and if one can share that simple meal with a loved one, in an aura of peace and love—one can forever be grateful. We *ought* to be!

During moments of whining, a *nudge* always happens.

Either a newspaper headline comes to sight about little babies being orphaned as both parents perish in an accident or in a riot or earthquake or a news about domestic violence or about how a terminal illness has wreaked havoc in a family or about how undertrials are languishing in jails in the most intolerable conditions or sometimes, a friend calls to share the news of an unexpected personal tragedy...

Obviously then, all my dejection about my articles and books getting rejected seem so very silly.

There are couples who have dream-weddings, but then a long string of dark days follows. And there are some who do not get married with the one they wanted to or the way they wanted their wedding to happen, but then lots of joys follow them the rest of their days. This is not to be mistaken as one inevitably leads to the other! The point is that some squares, after all, remain blank.

Can we predict/comprehend the empty squares?

Either a childhood is very protective and a pampered one or youth and the middle-ages are very fulfilling or old-age is at peace. No one can have all the phases and all the moments—all very happy and rosy indeed!

All that I write is just experience and observation. The working of this Universe cannot exactly be understood by us. Yes, not even very little of it! Most of the ways of this Universe are beyond our understanding and comprehension. *Why what happens; who gets what; who doesn't get anything and why not; and what happens with whom and why*—there is little point in trying to fathom it all. Everyone will have an opinion or some vague answers, based on the meagre experiences he or she has but truly speaking, no one has much clue of the real mechanism and how it works.

We must nevertheless, live as well as we can, with minimum strain or damage to one's mind, body and soul.

Hence, all of these talks, books and words. Just an attempt at sharing with one another. Came across this note written by an exasperated student:

Hey Buddy-Up-There,
We landed here pretty much
without any prior consent taken from us.
We accepted! Tried to live as well as we could...
Is there, however, a secret somewhere; some cryptic message somewhere which we are failing to decipher? Is there a message which if I could decode, I may get to choose the next (if there has to be) form of life and place where I shall swoop down and open my next mixed backpack?
Take your time, and send a signal
if you can...

When I look at the growing girls and boys around me, some of whom I get a chance to observe closely—for they are the growing kids of my friends and acquaintances, I wonder:

Ought I to envy them for they have an entire lifetime ahead of them? Or.... Or, ought I to pity them for they still have an entire lifetime ahead of them?

Would it be a gleeful adventure to have about 60 years more to live ahead? Or, am I truly glad from where I sit perched high up on the milestone of 49 years and know that I must somehow make it all work and hold myself together for just about 10 years more or preferably less?

Hmmmmmnnnn, I guess the latter looks good.

Of course, the young teenagers have more time at hand and they can plan their journeys to Mars (or even Venus, who knows) and they may have 5-D dining experiences or even greater speed in the digital world, and in all forms of transport and communication. But, other than these, I cannot much conjure up stuff to feel envious about.

They will be as clueless as we are or as our parents were. They too shall not know how to play the game of chess on the Board; how to unravel the back-pack of mixed deals they have on their shoulders. They too won't know which squares shall when be empty and why!

They are certainly not going to have stronger appetites, teeth, bones, ties (bonds), economies and governments! Yes, they could turn out to be far greater visionary and creative folks and we might miss seeing the consequences of all of that but then when I visualize the future state of our forests, rivers, roads, pesticide-laden foods, and the dimming glow of flora and fauna, all envy ebbs faraway.

Am I being unduly pessimistic?

It would be nice to be proven wrong and to be able to watch from up there—our girls and boys basking in warmth, joy and sense of ease. My worry is that, that sense of ease will be destroyed by the frightening speed at which excessive information spreads these days. However, no point in worrying. Every generation has had concerns and we all learn to live with what we have! Haven't all generations looked at their own with pride and sympathized with the next one?

No, not that I look at our times with pride and nor

do I envy the generation that preceded but in a relative sense, I feel we have lived better. Though a few squares were, are and shall always be empty...

We did not go through horrific wars and epidemics and natural and man-made disasters of horrendous magnitude. We have enjoyed the fruits of transport, communication, banking, trade—everything working faster and more efficiently. If we do shed a tear or two at the ties with loved ones turning shallow in this fast-paced world, we can take a pause and peep inside the basket full of sweet-sour memories of our younger days and smile!

The speed with which we have travelled, the ease with which we have bought and sold stuff online, the comfortable ways in which we have enjoyed tours n trips, multi-cuisine savories, entertainment in general—have been all good. We have seen times in our childhood when stuff that delighted us such as candies and street food was cheap and accessible to us all, and then of course, as we continue to cross our 40s, we have seen the cons of modern life too! To begin with, we had dedicated teachers and full-time parents, and wonderful memories of neighbors who cared and yet when the cons surfaced and we found them all meddlesome or authoritative, we rebelled in this very lifetime and licked for ourselves the sweet taste of privacy and independence. Our growing girls 'n guys will not know the sweet taste of privacy that is won after much rhetoric; of freedom that is fought and got.

The package is mixed for us all, irrespective of the times we were or are or will be born.

In this larger picture, at the micro level, it is true that

the package which we are handed down (called Life) is but a mixed bag... No matter how much attractive the package of somebody else looks, the ups and downs are all the same, except for their magnitude, colour, and the timings. It is never going to be a rosy path all the way for anybody and it is futile for us therefore, to seek so.

How much can we change what is given inside the package and how much of it is destiny, we might never know it accurately.

What to do, then?

Everybody's sensibilities are carved by his or her own instincts and experiences. Naturally, therefore, each one's conduct, character and reactions differ.

While one person may refuse to even accept that some squares are blank, some other may question as to why is it so and spend a life-time lamenting over his or her own blank squares. You or I may see injustice in this arrangement and decide to wage a battle against it. Some may calmly accept this truth as *fate,* and decide to procrastinate and wait for life to fill the empty squares.

Why not, at first, know which squares are empty and what is their impact on the quality of our life. For this, it is essential to know oneself. After all, we are all made up of some different stuff/composition altogether. While lack of food may rattle one, the lack of power may upset someone more forcefully.

Hence:

Step 1:

Know yourself. What stuff are you made up of? What will give you more fulfillment? What is your own definition of happiness?

Step 2:

Introspect. Observe which squares in your life are blank. List them.

Step 3:

Are the blank ones those that matter much to you? Will you be uneasy all throughout if they remain blank? Do not fight against all blank squares. Choose your battles wisely.

Step 4:

Are you prepared to challenge the status quo and fight it out? Struggle and slog to fill a particular vacant square?

Step 5:

Make a plan of action as to how do you propose to go about it. Do it.

Disclaimer:

There ought to be no regrets whatsoever. Gracefully accept what comes in the aftermath of such battles then.

Can all squares be filled if we make a strong resolve?

Do note that there will always be a few blank squares, about which we can do nothing.

If a child has never had the love of parents because they died or they divorced each other or they fight bitterly always,—there is nothing a child can do to fill that square. He or she will remain bereft of parental love. Similarly, if a couple is blessed with a *special child,* they can do nothing about it. Certain joys; certain special moments which other parents have with their kids, may be not there for them. However, they may have some other special moments with their blessed ones. Similarly, if one's loving life-partner is suddenly snatched away by death, there is no battle one can wage to fill that square with the same person again.

Wisdom, therefore, lies in knowing what one can change and what one can't! And wisdom lies in knowing which struggles to choose and to take the struggles how far.

I have seen many girls and boys who, in desperation, ended up with life-partners ill-suited to them. Life, became hell for them later. But they were looking at others and wanted to fill their kitty with a *wedding*, come what may. Whether a wedding or a car or a promotion or a desired posting or wooing love—there are people who are ready to turn the world upside down for filling up these blank squares. They go to any extent, in sheer exasperation. And then, they often wonder why are they not happy.

If there is no food in the house or if the roof needs repair or if one precious friendship is threatened by misunderstandings or if a kidney is failing—and then one gears up for the struggle to save or fill that square, it is understandable. However, people spend a lifetime collecting cars, brands, jewels, assets and the like! Thereafter, if peace or health or love eludes—they become cynical, and sigh: *life is unfair*!

Two years ago, Aamir (29) desperately wanted to get married since all of his friends were already married by then. He had a long wish-list though. Oblivious to facts such as: that he had a very modest job, a fiery temper and a mother who was strong and hot-headed, he, nevertheless kept rejecting proposals from girls who were dark or could not speak English fluently or who didn't meet other such frivolous parameters. After struggling for two years, he finally got married. The girl, as he desired, speaks English fluently, and has lovely hair, and eyes and is well-groomed. However, their world is no paradise; it is just trouble and trouble. The girl is hot-headed, stingy, unkempt, and careless. She wants to have more and more so that she can hoard it all and the mother-in-law will not allow that. The boy remains glum and depressed, caught as he always is—in a ferocious cross-fire.

All three of them wonder why life handed them a sore bargain!

It is not that we ought not to fall in love or not to try to find a suitable partner, but then a desperate hankering after what one believes is the key to one's happiness or obsessively pursuing that which one does not have and spending all days unhappily in the pursuit of that—usually does not lead to desired results.

If we think we can be happy only after we get one business deal or one more promotion or a bigger car or a swankier house or an attractive life-partner—we will never be truly happy. And soon, life will be over in a flash!!!

Those who know how to be reasonably contented and happy with the package deal (of a few empty and a few full squares) they have been endowed with—only those, I believe, allow *life* to play its own music and fill the squares at its own pace and as it deems fit.

They, then, remain at ease with themselves throughout their lives and live very well. Such people are a pleasure to be with, too.

Take a deep pause and think it over: Some squares shall always be blank! Can you live well with your blank ones?

If you are OK, at this moment, with what you don't have, you will live well at all times and in all situations.

Relax...

Spread the cheer!!!

□

And Thus...

There are days I feel very grateful and light.

I recall, in hindsight, that during all such days, I am very observant. When I observe keenly, I understand better.

There are days when either a written word or a spoken sentence or a marvelous action of someone tugs happily at my sleeve and I feel thrilled.

And then, there are those days when nothing appeals; no wise word matters and all seems dreary. I wonder then that what is the use of millions of books, hymns and sermons when our conduct and character as human beings are not any better over the years? Disillusionment simply engulfs the whole being.

Does it happen with you?

There are days when a lot of thoughts and ideas yearn to stumble out of the heart and tumble down on paper...

And then there are days when I wonder why I write and of what use is all this writing going to be? Who is going to read and who shall recall and what difference will it make to anyone or to me—whether now or even when I am dead and gone?

And then there are days in between all of the above days, when I smile; feel amused and utter a chuckle! For in all of the varied kind of days, are hidden all the crucial cryptic messages.

Although there are all kinds of days, certain realizations remain unflinching:

A few wise words always matter...

They help in handling a bit of the turmoil that dark clouds bring! Even on days when wise words (heard or read earlier) don't matter, they remind us that finally, there are no forever solutions to anything! Anyone who writes or claims or preaches that: *'come to me or read this book and all your problems will be solved or that you will feel no sorrow or pain hereafter'* is a terrible liar or a shrewd merchant.

(I suggest: try and stay away from all those lofty books and condescending life-coaches telling us to detach ourselves or rise above the mundane idiosyncrasies of this world).

When nothing matters, we must remember that we have to actually live every phase in entirety and that there are going to be no short-cuts or formulae that will transform a sorrow into a joy.

We must cry at times; feel dreary at times; jubilant and joyous at other times; calm on some days and ruffled on other days; at ease on some days and in turmoil on some other days.

My simple conclusions are:

- **We are a mixed bag. Life, too, is a mixed package deal. Just as no person can be only**

good or only bad, so also no life can be only dark or only sunny and bright.

- **We can try to live reasonably well and wisely, but no one can live perfectly; flawlessly.**
- **No one has any special answers or any secret formula to enable you to live better. All are just guessing...or selling us stuff!**
- **Life and People are not always clearly apparent, all at once. Not much is as it seems! Wait. Pause. There are many threads, facets and shades beyond the obvious!**

An old wise fable goes thus:

Once upon a time, there was a monk travelling through a village's market, along with his four disciples. They suddenly spotted a man who was dragging his cow with a rope. The cow didn't want to move but the man was forcibly trying to make it walk towards home. Over the next several minutes, the monk and his disciples saw that the cow had not moved an inch. Others too had gathered to watch the spectacle.

The monk asked his disciples: "Tell me who is bound to whom?" One of the younger disciples replied: "Well, it is clearly the cow which is bound to the man.

The man is the master since he is holding the rope and the cow must follow him wherever the man takes her. The monk was amused with the answer. He said: "Now, watch this," and saying so—he took out a pair of scissors from his bag and cut the rope. As soon as he cut the rope, the cow ran away and the man started to run after his cow.

The monk looked at the intrigued faces of the young learners and asked them: "Now, what do you see? Who is bound to whom? Who is the master now? The cow is not interested in the man. In fact, it is trying to escape. It is the man who is bound to her and is therefore running after his cow."

The monk continued: "Not much is as it seems, always. Try to look deeper. We too carry a lot of garbage inside our minds and we think that the thoughts want to occupy our mind. But, it is not so. All the nonsense is not interested in us. We are interested in holding on to the garbage. If you cut the rope and release the unnecessary garbage, it will run away from you."

- **Finally, nothing matters. It doesn't matter if you are rich or poor; if you are ugly or beautiful; if you are famous or not; if you have attended fine universities and read books or if you are an illiterate. The state of the mind is simply not connected to any of these. All of us who have come here, will have to simply open his or her own mixed bundle and handle whatever comes out of the bundle and simply depart at the destined time and in the destined way.**

□□□